A QUICK *Kiss* OF REDEMPTION

A QUICK *Kiss* OF
REDEMPTION

& Other Stories

David Means

WILLIAM MORROW AND COMPANY, INC.   *NEW YORK*

*The author would like to give special
thanks to his editor,
Douglas Stumpf, and to his agent, Mary Evans,
and finally, to his friend of
twenty-five years, Neal Anderson.*

Copyright © 1991 by David Means

"For Hani, Aged Five, That She Be Better Able to Distinguish a Villain," by Gene Baro, copyright © 1951, 1979 by The New Yorker, Inc. Used by permission.

Recognizing the importance of preserving what has been written, it is the policy of William Morrow and Company, Inc., and its imprints and affiliates to have the books it publishes printed on acid-free paper, and we exert our best efforts to that end.

Library of Congress Cataloging-in-Publication Data

Means, David.
   A quick kiss of redemption & other stories / David Means.
     p. cm.
   ISBN 0-688-09459-7
   I. Title.
   [PS3563.E19505 1991]
   813'.54—dc20   90-19559
                                             CIP

Printed in the United States of America

First Edition

1 2 3 4 5 6 7 8 9 10

BOOK DESIGN BY LISA STOKES

To Genève

Contents

Contents

A QUICK *Kiss* OF
REDEMPTION

The
Myth
of
Devotion

Arrival in a foreign land is easy; we fall into it, step down from the plane into the dry, hot air. No effort was made by us to arrive at this place; we did not have a long voyage across the sea by steamer, or even a long train journey, to validate or give charm to our arrival. In a small rental car we move—jet lagged and weary—through the coastal towns, along a road that curls up into the mountains briefly before it cuts back to the sea, then back inland until the road ends in a long, straight path across a scrubby, lifeless bit of land so familiar we hardly look, even though it *is* another country, a place that should amaze us after the long, cold winter months in New York.

Our apartment is unchanged, white, square, perched on a small terrace of stone above the town. As we pull up, mangy dogs chase our tires. They greet us as if we left a week ago. No one is around. It's late afternoon; therefore, people are all still down at the beach taking in sun, which is still strong.

With a twist of the big skeleton key, the heavy doors moan open. Dark and cool, unused since our last visit, the apartment has been suspended in time. Exactly where we left them on the coffee table, the old paperbacks curl from last year's sun and salt.

We throw all the windows wide open, letting the light kill the past. While Nicholas unlocks the padlocks from the cupboard upstairs and pulls down snorkels, fins, and towels still covered with last year's sand and white swirls of dried salt, I rinse the dust off the mismatched dishes in the kitchen. I stare at them under the water. The sink is built too low, and water splashes on my knees. The rubber smell of the fins and snorkels reaches all the way downstairs; it reminds me of condoms, of surgical tubing, plastic garbage bags.

That evening our Dutch friend Brogan comes over with a bottle of cheap wine to fill us in on the year's gossip. The sun has moved down behind the apartment. As we drink on the roof, I notice my husband's silence. Behind his head, I see the piled apartments of the village below us, and a sea the color of dried blood.

"The girls are still good," Brogan says, jiggling his bushy yellow eyebrows at Nicholas, and avoiding my eyes. Absurdly messed up, his brilliant gold hair gives him the gentle look of some kind of Einstein, whose concerns reach far beyond this world. Brogan's genius, though—if one could call it that—is rooted in his ability to spot a half-naked girl a mile away, to idle away the remaining years of his life in a state of high erotic energy.

"There is still one who is the queen of the beach," he nods, slipping out of his formal English. "And they vear their tops without tops."

"Topless," I say.

"Yes."

"An the boys vollow her every ver."

"As usual."

A gentle smile breaks over Nicholas's mouth; he does a wicked good imitation of Brogan's voice: snide, perfect, out of the corner of his mouth like a clown.

Brogan goes over my body with his eyes, marbled blue above swirling white, a strange reverse of magazine photos of planet earth. Against the white roof, in the fading light, I strain to see into them. I am too tired. The trip was long. The land is too brown and dusty this year.

"He hugs too much," I once complained about Brogan, and he does, wrapping his arms around you, kissing each cheek and then doing it again.

The next morning we walk to the beach. The town square is still charming, littered with white and red ice cream and bubble gum wrappers. Slouched in lawn chairs, a few old men, retired from fishing, lounge in the packed dust. One nods at us familiarly but remains quiet. Neither tourists nor Spaniards, we hardly exist. Each year we come. It has been that way forever. There are science-fiction shows on the town's single television set, suspended over the bar down on the beach, that explain our glittery materialization out of nothing.

On the beach the young native fishermen parade, displaying their rich tans and muscles, the result of pulling nets. The beach is short. There isn't much room. A few women are topless. Seeing them, Nicholas winces and pops his eyes, trying to be comic about his staring.

One girl is prancing devoid of all modesty. One cannot miss her. She devours the whole beach while from behind sunglasses and newspapers, under the shadows of beach umbrellas, the men watch.

Nicholas shifts his thighs to adjust his swimsuit.

As we take in the sun, the girl—known universally this year as the Queen—flounces and preens and draws to her side a small, international entourage of young men, boys, really: two lean, black-haired Italians with sailboards; a French kid with orange surfer trunks down to his knees and a blasé expression; and alongside these dark tans, a British boy whose freckles are splayed like leopard spots across his skin, which is burned red in places as if he had been slapped.

The boys dance on the stage of their desire, keeping a certain distance from her body as if getting too close might result in a massive explosion, a gigantic explosion, a massive chain reaction. One dribbles a soccer ball to another; one runs down to the water and backflips himself into an oncoming wave.

The Queen lies still on her back, an island of flesh.

Nicholas rolls over to speak to me scientifically. He is, after all, a physicist. The way the boys move around the girl reminds him of the habitual hangout spots of electrons and their random strays. There is also a tug, he explains, an attraction between hydrogen and hydrogen that holds water together, and, as a result, the entire world.

"You're making some elaborate metaphors out of nothing," I insist, wondering where that "nothing" has come from.

"That's exactly what I'm talking about," he says. "Making something from nothing. Do you see how close they get.

Never too close. All of that energy focused just around her body."

"She's a girl with a lot of boyfriends," I explain. I look at his fluorescent green swimming suit. An old Stetson, deformed from the sun, is pulled down over his brow.

Later, she goes in swimming. She slips through the surface, splashes up, gathers her hair into a bundle, squeezes it dry with both hands, chin to the sky, water kissing her throat. Nicholas watches over the top of his book, *Quantum Phenomena*.

That night we gather together with people we see each year. It is getting late. Polishing off our "final" bottle of wine, we finger plates of fried calamari.

Is a baby due soon? someone wonders. Nicholas explains that we are trying hard to get one in the works. "In the works." I am sure those were his exact words.

Brogan ignores this and brings up the name of the girl, the Queen. It sounds as smooth as a ripe pear. Nicholas bites into it by saying it again.

"She's from Madrid but her mother is French so her name is Chloe," Brogan explains in the light of the naked bulb, his face old and wrinkled.

I am happy to see him tired and weak, hunched over the wooden table as he describes a young girl.

"She's the one this year with the boys," Clark states in his nasal, flat Cleveland accent. For as long as I've known him, he has always had a cigar or pipe between his fingers or in his mouth. "They come and go every year," he says offhandedly. Kindly, he rests his doggish eyes on me.

And then she walks by with a boy at her side, arches against the blinking slot machine across the room, extends her brown arm out against the ceramic wall. The same light that ages Brogan's face turns hers a rich brown.

The boy plays each coin carefully, or pretends to. His eyes fix on the spinning indicators, attempting to make a skill luck. It works. He wins, and the machine pipes electric music as the heavy pesetas clunk into the lip.

A gray tattooed fish, hidden in the dark tones of his bicep, jumps as he pulls the lever again; again, the fruits fall magically together, the electric ditty plays, and there is a burst of more coins.

The man/boy is beautiful. He knows the tricks. His long body holds answers. For so long we have tried to catch the graceful luck he holds in his arm. To get the fruit in the wrong order would be impossible with him.

They waltz around the stiffback chairs cinematically, like Rita Hayworth and Fred Astaire, knowing we are watching them.

"I feel jealous," Nicholas slurs.

"Fuck you," I say. But I feel it too.

Walking back to the apartment through the dark, I remember a night, last year, when the moonless sky was splattered with stars. We lay naked and drunk on the flat roof, listening to the sound of the waves traveling the great distance from the beach.

"Let's make life, let's make life," I prayed into his ear.

"I want a baby."

Both of us had it in our minds that all we had to do was drive into each other hard enough. We flung and kicked until our skin became red and raw, our backs chalked with whitewash.

When we could no longer go on, he reached down and wiped a tear from my eye. I brushed the white marks from his back.

"The gypsies are still down at their campfire," I whispered. You could hear their throaty singing if you listened hard enough.

"The hell they are."

I felt slim and elegant standing in the cool air, naked, at the edge of the terrace. Two dogs bayed mournfully at each other.

Touching my fingers, he pulled me down gently and cradled me.

It was our last attempt.

We drive in the morning through the desert to the weekly market in Carboneras. On both sides of the road eroded *mesetas* rise up, mountainous, and flatten against the sky. The road cuts down into the *ramblas*, the riverbed, crusted with gray winter mud and boulders. If rain came suddenly, we would be washed away in the torrent.

When we reach the crossroads, I turn the wrong way and take the twisting one-lane strip of old asphalt up to the lighthouses, shifting the car with sharp, controlled jabs, bringing the engine into low gear.

For a moment, as I work around a curve, we look down at the crumbled edge and feel suspended midair. I hear Nicholas gasp. I think about going over. I wonder how it would feel to fall.

But at the top the road opens up into a wide sheet of dirt. To the left is the new lighthouse, freshly whitewashed, with a shiny, modern dome—an emerald green helmet of glass and black metal. To the right squats the thousand-year-old Moor tower.

Beyond the parking area, the land falls away into a deep pit. The core of the mountain is gone, strip-mined.

"Spanish law allows them only to mine the inside of the mountain," I remind him, "and leave the outside standing."

At the base of the old tower, we look down at the sea—morning colors of oxidized copper green with blue around the edges of reefs. Fishing boats far out in the water look like shavings of wood. In the cliffs are the small, dangerous alcoves where swimmers go to have privacy and drown in the weird influxes of current.

Our village, barely holding on to the slope of land, is a splatter of white confetti.

I say into the wind, "This is a lonely spot, isn't it?"

"Yes it is," he answers, blankly.

"To see the whole thing at once and so far away."

A few days later, on Friday, the sea has a sharp, fine chop of current.

With expert strokes the boy rows her across the beachfront to his fishing boat. Even from the distance, I can see the long muscles that web his shoulders.

She climbs up first. He places his hand on the small of her back, helping. Bright ribbon flags bend on long poles at the stern, and nets overflow from a wooden box on the deck. It's a fat, ugly boat. On the deck is a small shack forecastle the size of a phone booth, topped with a long antenna, a cone-shaped loudspeaker, tangles of wires, and a tiny Spanish flag.

The Queen positions herself on the bow wearing only a pair of white bikini bottoms, a translucent strand of fabric. In the wind, her hair flutters out. Defying gravity, her breasts curve upward. I believe her body is as perfect as any woman could want.

Once he gets the engine going, sputtering a cloud of blue fumes, they swing out past the last crop of rocks and disappear into the coves of our imaginations, with hidden beaches and the sealike smell of sex. The whole beach seems to sigh.

Beside me, Nicholas has his legs squeezed together; for a long time he sits silently, tight-mouthed, as if sucking on a hard candy.

That evening, a wind comes off the sea through the reed mat walls and swings the bare bulbs. Shadows move. Faces change shape.

Brogan leans back and holds a *perron* above his head to pour a tiny stream of wine into his mouth. This is a horrible, animal way to drink.

With amazement, a nameless British couple at our table watch him. They've been drinking since early afternoon.

"I'd say her voice has a curve to it, an inner tone, a fine, voody, reedy quality like that of an oboe," Brogan says, licking the red from his lips.

"But her singing voice is rough and loud," Nicholas adds, lighting one of Brogan's stubby little cigars, rolling the tip in the match flame.

"What's this?" the British man says, bewildered. His face is ruddy and flat; he is the kind of guy who would gladly brawl to the death in the soccer stands. All of us wonder how he got down here in the first place. Offensively ugly, his wife has allowed the wide straps of her suit to rub raw blisters in her sunburnt skin, which she is shedding like a snake. She belches slightly, catches herself.

Brogan inhales another stream of wine and begins talking. "But she could vhisper a tune beautifully. And she loves to smile. During the vinter months in Madrid, she has been known to spend hours in the mirror practicing, curling her lips, baring her teeth. Because, really, it is a useful smile she has. Really, it is. She could vin the world vith that smile."

"In what way?" Nicholas pretends to wonder.

"Ah ho ho," Brogan chuckles, "maybe I should not describe it. Yes? Maybe not here in this company. Ah, but ve have all seen vhat that smile can do, haven't ve, really?"

"Let's change the subject," I say.

"Oh, by all means, continue," the British man grunts. I notice a strange curve to his cheek, as if he'd recently been stitched up around his mouth.

On the television behind the battered zinc bar, a basketball game is on. Tiny figures sprint one way and then another.

"Maybe your wife is right. It is a bit strange," Brogan says. "That we should devote ourselves to the task of figuring out Chloe."

"Not all of us are up to the task, or even care much."

"But," Nicholas says, "it's such an interesting phenomenon to see one woman on the beach become the all-consuming object of desire. And there are so many others on the beach who could do the same thing if—"

"It's that *if*." Brogan pokes the empty *perron*.

"What 'if'?" the Englishman wonders, stupefied.

I lift my glass up and speak, keeping my eye on Brogan. "I don't think it's that complicated. You wish there was some mysterious thing. But she's just a kid. You old boys like to think the kind of things you're thinking, make her into something she's not. She flatters your male vanity because she cares that you watch her. She is not a myth. She's a kid."

"Ho ho ho, you think so do you?" Brogan's face flushes red, embarrassed. His English improves as he gets drunk.

"Drink up," Nicholas says, breaking in.

As I get up to leave, the Englishman becomes inspired and rambles about the Blitz. Walking into the darkness, the lights behind me, I hear him explain, "V-one bombers hobbled over so slowly that, sometimes, a farmer would pick one off with his own hunting rifle in his very own field. Just like that. Often the things would buzz over on the way to London. Headless planes without pilots."

"Good God," Nicholas said, "what the hell are you talking about?"

"We were working on our own rockets at the time. I believe the Krauts picked up the idea from us."

On Monday night the wind starts quickly, comes down from the mountains without mercy like spring melt-off. We wake to the clatter of the window shutters banging ferociously. Nicholas goes upstairs to batten them down, leaving me alone in bed.

The wind does not ebb and flow; it is an unyielding blast, one that will last for days, drown the town, hide the sound of my footsteps as I sneak upstairs to see what my husband is up to.

Hidden in the dark, I watch him through the window of the guest bedroom as he moves across the smooth roof. Staring into the darkness, he lifts a pair of binoculars to his eyes. Beyond the edge of the balcony, two pink streetlights are haloed with dust. The rest of the town is dark.

All he can see, I'm sure, is a formless fuzzy nothing, the spray of blood from the back of his eyelids. Getting closer might help. He leans forward. The starlight turns his back purple.

He berates himself for staring into the darkness with an old pair of field glasses. He knows he's looking into nothing. Nothing is what he wants to see, I think.

When he turns to the side I see the shadow of his erection. Lightly, he traces it with the tips of his fingers.

He sits down against the wall with his legs apart. I see

him only from the chest up. His arms move slightly forward
and back, as if he's rowing a boat out into the sea.

Back downstairs, I wait for him in bed. The wind is dry,
cool, and saltless, composed of chalky, inland dust. Lying on
the sheets, I feel my skin sticky with dust. When he comes
back, he smells like salt. His legs are sticky with sweat.

On Sunday morning she's back, alone, on her reed
mat, wearing a new one-piece swimming suit cut low in
the back with blue pinstripes. To bare her chest she has
rolled the suit down. The beach is crowded with families.
Her entourage remains aloof and far down the sand. They
will not easily forgive her adventure with a village fisherman. Still, at times, kicking a ball or tossing a disk, they turn
to watch her.

In an hour she becomes the Queen again; a few boys
move along the water's edge to play paddleball for her ben-
efit, popping an occasional hit in her direction, splashing
and diving for the ball.

My husband is watching with a new, devout intensity;
his eyes are massaging her body.

My eyes go over *his* body. Two weeks of swimming
have toned his muscles. He looks good, tight and firm.

Nicholas is thinking to himself: Where is ecstasy to be
found if not here? What is the price of such desire?

Rubbing the elastic between his leg and his balls, he
pretends he can imagine the little space where the land slips
under the water—a space probably less than a molecule
thick—which reminds us, subconsciously, of the way things
end and begin amid the stuff of life: sand, salt, seaweed,
lime, pearls.

The fisherman struts down the beach, stops, and stands
over the Queen with his legs spread apart. She blinks up at

him. The tattoo on his arm quivers. The wind blows his words away from us.

The standoff lasts a few seconds. The Queen shakes her head no. None of the boys watching this spectacle, water lapping their feet, dare confront him. He stands firm, black hair fluttering in his eyes, arms tight to his side; until, quickly, he lifts one arm up and, at the same time, as if responding to his own movement, he uses the top of his foot to pick up sand and kick it in her face.

Sand rings her mouth like a clown. On his knees, taking hold of her hair in a clump, he yanks her head back.

Immobile with horror, I see his single finger trace a line across her neck, ear to ear, leaving a thin red scratch. She shoves him away; he stumbles back, pushes his hair out of his eyes, spits into the sand and stomps off up the beach.

She cries as she spits the sand from her mouth into her palm.

Nicholas jumps up, stumbles across the sand, and hovers over her as she rubs the sand from her lips with a towel. She doesn't understand a word of his English, so he tries his ragged Spanish. Her tiny raisin-shaped nipples are not equipped for nursing a child, and her tight, brown stomach is as smooth as plastic. When I see his arm go to her shoulder, I turn away from them to face the cliffs where the Guardia Civil once hid in caves to spy on the beach. Back then, nudity was a serious crime resulting in a nudge with the tip of a submachine gun and fines, trials, judgment, punishment.

I think I will miss the landscape more than anything; the simplicity of the emptiness; the way the roads fade from asphalt to dirt, to ruts, to endless circles. I console myself with the fact that I am not the only one who was forced from the land. I think of the Moors; I think of those who died on the same road I'll use to get to the airport. On that road, Franco machine-gunned mothers and children as they fled Malaga.

Brogan consoles me. I hate his voice, but know he's trying to be sympathetic.

"Are you leaving tomorrow?"

"Yes."

"And he is staying?"

"Yes. It looks like it."

I wait for him make a pass at me. His nature tells him I need a man. I would like a reason to smash his rutty, sun-baked face.

We are on the roof together. We can't see the stars because I have the light on. Wasps have built a nest over the bulb, and you can see the combs swarming with dazed lar-vae. The black insects swoop around us. Brogan nurses a sting on his arm, but I refuse to turn the light off. The wind is gone. He peels another cigar. I leave him and go in to pack my things. The field glasses are mine. I remember buying them in a sporting goods store in Maine from a man in a plaid cap and red vest who explained they were excellent for deer and moose too. I remember his face, red, splotched with veins, his teeth gone.

On the plane, air howls through the spigots over my head. The engines rev and shake. It's a shaky world, Nicholas used to say, referring to all the sensitive instru-ments his physics experiments required. Tell me about it, I would answer. His favorite piece of equipment is a two-ton hydraulic-footed lead table needed to keep his equipment stable. It is a heavy, serious piece of equipment. I've seen it many times in many places. He drags it from university to university like a favorite piano. The workers would set it up, and the instruments on it would hum, draw laser light the color of ruby into crystals. From the air, he'd gather his answers.

A man in ear protectors looks under the wing. He reminds me of a public television science show I once saw. Doctors implanted a device in a deaf girl's ear—a tiny electrode the size of a cuff button laid against her eardrum. Closed off in a glass booth, next to an electronic monitoring box, a scientist adjusted a dial and, for the first time, she heard the hard crackle of sound floating across her mind. She opened her eyes wide and jiggled her head. Again the doctor adjusted the dial, rolling it between his fingers. As if looking for the sound waves, she opened her eyes wide, until the whites were clearly visible; listening, she looked dazed and alone.

Salvation

Not one of us had the slightest notion of caring one bit, or listening to what Sis's new boyfriend wanted to say, except, of course, for Sis, who had a vested interest—shall we say—in his words. What with his having the kind of bright red hair you just had to ignore—an indigenous shock of color illuminated from within—and all the freckles to go with it, splotches of them looking like ink spills on his arms and cheeks. And that voice. All slurry, filled up with the kind of ripe little slips Daddy so hated. Matter of fact, Daddy had him pegged as a loser from the start as far as I could see, put down on the list with all the others.

Later, when the fight bloomed among Sis, Momma, and
Daddy, my foregone conclusion would be confirmed.
Daddy would slam his hand down on the chopping counter
in the kitchen and call the boy a loser, scum of the earth,
not worth a shit, a twerp. Mother, her arms amputated by
the suds in the sink, would throw her head back and get all
soggy faced, unable to brush the tears.

There was a unique logic in Sis's choices of guys. She
had a kind of acute ability—and I do think it a skill of
sorts—of making the wrong choice in men. Her selections
were pulled through the family like a piece of thread
through a wound, and in a strange way they held things
together like that.

A sort of lazy, half-religious, post-Christmas feeling set-
tles down over the living room. I think of it as a Christ-Mess.
A burnt log sizzles grotesquely in the grate. A few brushes of
snow collect on the windowsills.

Daddy's sunk into his leather easy chair with one of
those rechargeable screwdrivers—a gift from Grandpa
Gates—in his hand. He's holding it up and letting it spin,
screaming like a dentist drill while Mother, prim and proper
in her wing-back chair, goes through her description of lit-
tle-girl Christmases she used to have, years ago, in a house
only about two miles from ours.

While Momma gets into the bit about the tire chains
and the hard depression times, when a turkey was a big, big
deal, Leo's red hair is flaming all over the place and you can
tell he just wants to talk, bad, like some convicted murderer
waiting to make a last statement of some sort. Leo's got an
outdated haircut that would make a marine proud, right
down to the bare naked scalp on the sides; and his dark
green eyes look like furniture coasters, big and emerald
green. Sis's running her fingers over his head, bristling like
Velcro.

The tree's doing an epileptic blink-a-thon. Daddy's still driving invisible screws. Leo's slicking his lips with his own spit, readying up to say something. Sis is working her fingers over his hair. Mom is still talking on about tire chains, the sound they make at night on a snowy road. Wrapping paper is scrunched in balls on the floor. The spirit of the Lord pushes hard down upon us, heavy, like a usual Sunday, but worse.

"Momma," I say. "Momma, Leo has something to say."

A wet-mop silence falls over the room—the screwdriver stops and Momma's story is cut short around sleigh rides—while Leo gives me this nice look with his big eyes.

I know what he's working up to, making his lips slippery with his tongue, swaying the green of his eyes over the living room, the light blue super plush wall-to-wall carpet, Daddy with his screwdriver lofted up now like a saber ready to plunge, Momma still dreary with thoughts of sleighs, depressing turkeys.

That afternoon Leo and I had gone out for a hike. We threw snowballs at each other. He taught me how to spit-freeze a lick of your hair into weird shapes.

He said to me, slipping the words around his broken teeth, "I just may run on home to South Dakota with that sister of yours. Guy has got to see a bit of his family at one time or another, and I have an inkling to do so right now."

His kind I know well, I figure, so I listen up close, the sting of snow flicking my cheeks. Sis had so many guys you had to wonder where they all came from, and what dark vein she mined to get them, what kind of sinkhole—as Daddy called it—she pulled them out of. Most were the kind of guys you saw hanging at some dingy franchise burger joint at two in the morning making patterns in the spilled salt, drawing hard on a vanilla shake—wondering, just wondering.

"I got family," he insists, slapping the back of my head. "I got plenty of them out there. Sam, Joe, Morris B., Ruby, Honora, and Little Jen. Couple of years ago when Sam lived here, we all had a reunion of sorts right here when Big Johnny lived here. Took up a whole section of Maple Park, at least ten picnic tables. Later we stacked them up on top of each other, about fifteen or so, into a pyramid of sorts, and made the paper the next day with a big headline: VANDALS STACK TABLES."

Both of us start laughing about this. I give him a smile because already I figure that pie-in-the-sky dream he has forming, of taking Sis rolling out to some other state, will get about as far as the county line, if there even *is* a county line.

"I've got family," he says. "I do."

Fact was I knew where he was living, and it was no place for family, or much else for that matter—down near the defunct Amtrak station, amid the red-brick rubble of the wax paper factory, in a room with Magic Marker writing on the walls: peace symbols, dirty slang, names of other boys like Leo who had come through.

What family he did have would mean nothing to anyone later. He'd be running wild again, off to some other place or girl. I knew that. He probably knew it, deep down. But for the duration of our walk he pretty much settled the point with me. And I was willing as anyone, or more so, to follow along with his attempt at taking Sis away.

So when he licks his lips and begins talking to all of us, I'm fully aware of the direction we're heading.

"Before I start, Mr. Williams, Mrs. Williams, I want to thank you folks for about the nicest Christmas time I have ever had away from my family folks. That dinner Mrs. Williams was, honestly, about the best yet for me, honest."

A kind of half-moon motherly smile, unresisting, forms all over Momma's face, being not one to pull back from her duties as a care provider; that face would change, soon, I knew, at the mere mention of her daughter's name, and especially at the implication of movement out of state.

Daddy has one of the sergeant-to-private, don't-mess-with-me-boy stares he has perfected to an art since his stint in Korea. The screwdriver doesn't help much, either.

"You all know I got family folk here and there. All over the place, actually." He laughs his sweet chuckle, trying hard to smooth his voice out into something acceptable. "Coast to coast, as they say. Matter of fact, I brought some photos I thought you'd like to take a look at, while we're in the spirit and all."

In what takes about ten seconds, we realize we're in for a first of some kind. Finally, we might get a good look into the deep, dark void, the seeding ground for the likes of guys like Leo.

With long fingers, he opens the small album—the cheap kind you get free at Fotomat—onto his knees. Sticky plastic pages charged up with static, he pulls them apart. We move campfire close, gather up around his knees in a bunch. Even Daddy's scrunched down on his big legs as if he wouldn't miss it for anything, still holding that dead-cold stare for insurance along with the screwdriver. Both knees beneath her, Momma sits like a little girl.

The first page has a photo of four raggedly dressed kids looking like they're ready to be shot, nailed down with sad pouts on a saggy old front porch. Next to them, a lady in a gray apron firms herself with a scolding look. Behind them, summer heat flays out with dustweed and gnats twirling, and far past the house, around the photo's edges, is an old horizon you can tell isn't anywhere near our house because it seems tight and straight enough to cut somebody.

"That's me, Sam, Joe, little Jen, and Momma, and Big Johnny," Leo says, all tight in the throat. "If I recollect, Morris B. took this photograph."

Daddy's puckering his face a bit as if some bad smell blew out of the picture.

Sis keeps her eyes right up into Leo's, catches the greens of them with her smile, making lovely lips at him as if she'd suck his face dry right there with Daddy hunching and Momma blushing embarrassed over the decrepit old Polaroids showing a bunch of tattered rags caught on the fence of life.

"That one's in Branchville," Leo's saying, "right here in this state, outside of Detroit where we lived for a time. Near as I can recollect, Big Johnny took that one cause that's Morris B. with the sweatshirt draped over his shoulder."

The house looks the same as the others, falling into itself as if the nails had popped out, as gray as driftwood. While we look, the drone of Leo's voice pushes names around quick and defensive, piling them up as if to prove his existence any way he can; names tacked on with letters like secret codes—a long stack of people he's touched, Sammy P., Ricky M., Little Sam; and all seemingly related, woven into the family somehow—a bunch of hangers-on and latchkey slobs; Daddy's face says so much as he listens.

For a time we're all caught in our hard-locked smiles, so hard with pity our jaws are aching. Even Daddy's smiling his head off, loosening up his face. But it firms up hard again when Leo hits the grand finale: Sis's face appearing out of nowhere amid the last page of photographs! There she is surrounded by the overexposed yellow shots of keggers and summer picnics. Both of them, staggering against each other, looking ever so much like the rest, with the old wax paper factory lurking behind, crumbling red bricks, and the low clouds scrubbing down between the listing smoke-stacks. Wild-eyed, she looks ready to skip off, to join ranks with the faces in the pages.

Seeing Sis in the photo album sends Momma back across the room to her chair; Daddy looms over the two of them in his military stance. His eyes wander up to his Purple Heart, mounted in a velvet display stand on the mantel.

Launching deeper into the sloppy voice that Daddy hates, desperation leaking all over his words, Leo sets to explaining things and digs himself deeper in doing so; he does not know it, but by that point, the photos have tried and convicted him, nailed his case shut.

"I'd love to have a second Christmas visit with all of them, or at least my Momma," he says, "'cepting of course it would be out there with Big Jen in South Dakota or thereabouts. And I'd really like it if Kate could come along with me."

I'm watching the big pools of blood filling Daddy's cheeks and the drop of his jaw down. Momma is readying to cry out from her place on the couch.

Daddy goes down behind the tree, bristling the branches, and yanks the plug from the socket so it dies— a flat dark blue spruce devoid of all meaning; then he spins himself toward them as if to spit the blood right out of his cheeks.

This little puppy look comes over Leo's face. He casts it right at me because he thinks I'm somehow on his side, but I'm not, not after the ratty lineup of faces he's shown us.

"No, sir," Daddy's voice comes out flat as a bark.

"Sir," Leo says formally, waiting for permission to speak.

"Yes?"

"Can't you all take the Christmas spirit and such into your heart at this moment?"

"Son, you ever think maybe I don't want my daughter, who is only sixteen years of age, going all the way out to South Dakota with a deek like you?"

"I got family, sir. She'd be safe with me."

"Son, you've got family spread out like the plague," Daddy says. The electric screwdriver twists in his hand as he points it out before him.

"No. You get your sorry little ass into your coat and out of this house right this minute, Son. Right now."

Sis moves herself away from Leo a foot or two.

Leo begins to say something, but changes his mind, the screwdriver being too much for him.

Leo lifted himself up and left the house on his own will and volition. Momma disappeared out to begin clanking pots. Daddy replugged the tree and spent a good long time flicking the screwdriver and making a study of the blinking lights. Sis took to her room for the usual crying scene, soaking up her pillow so she could show me it later, a testament to her anguish.

While she was crying, on account of it, Daddy located the album and did not hesitate to put it onto the smoldering log in the fireplace, setting it carefully, where it sat for a while before the heat built up and in a pop it burst out all orange and purple, the plastic pages finally released of static and curling, bubbling, brown like syrup.

I missed Leo's eyes and imagined him walking alone all the way back to his room through the old, gray snow, passing the colorful strings of house lights, trees ablaze behind sheer curtains, the bottoms of his boots leaking snow. I imagined that already the pain of his loss was fading like heat seeping from the attic rafters, wisping away into the dark, clear sky. He probably had little desire to take my sister anywhere, really, except to bed. If he could swing a big net around the country and collect them all, then maybe he'd have some family to call his own. But that wasn't likely. And without family, as far as I can see, you're nothing at all.

The
Library
of
Desire

lipping is an exactitude, a sacred removal of information from magazines, newspapers, brochures, comic books, handouts. The clips are each folded up, or cut into three-by-four-inch squares. He left little room for deviation. The information in his library was all contained in shoe boxes from a store down the street, Seattle's largest budget shoe store; he had an agreement with the manager who let him have as many as he wanted. The folded packets were arranged two rows per box, separated by a sheet of cardboard or paper.

Piled to the ceiling, against the walls of the dingy room, the shoe boxes form a narrow vault, leaving just enough room for the sheet of corduroy on which my uncle slept. The floor sags and some of the boxes have jiggled loose, ready to tumble down from their stacks; the building has been condemned, or damned, by the City of Seattle—by order of the mayor no less—to be restored to twenty two-bedroom "units." A gray neon sign in the window downstairs twists to the word Woody's, a name I can remember Uncle mentioning during his visits to Ohio.

A tough nut to crack. Where to begin. I sit and begin to look at the stacks themselves. Another batch of boxes is stored elsewhere, in a warehouse, someplace, in Chicago, I think. But for now I just look at the boxes and the numbers on the side: beginning with the decayed ones in the room's left-hand corner: 00010:57001, to 00010:57002: but then 00010:57098 as you move down the stack. The numbers are in black ballpoint ink.

Baseball scores, the Dewey decimal system, the Library of Congress, anything at all might be nice, I think; certitude, some insight of order; from the first stack to the second the numbers go from 00010 to 00888. I cross my legs and take a seat in the center of the room where an unfinished box lies. The box on the floor reminds me that whenever he visited us in the Midwest, he came with a box and began a file for that trip. I scan the stacks for something I recognize, lodged in my memory, a color, a flick of print, anything.

Inside the box on the floor, the numbers and headings go across the top, either on the clipped packet themselves, or on an index card, like a file: There are a few names I don't know, Doughterly 345-889-0; Weeland 565-889-5. Many are just numbers, and my own name. I pull that packet out and begin to unfold the contents onto the floor. The letter I wrote—000-789-6—a few months ago about the book, about the stories I was writing. Uncle Russell has underlined my own words: "*The leaves come down quickly here, change suddenly, in a flash, because you don't see them really. One day you just go to Riverside Park and they've changed. Another day you go and they're all gone, sucked up by the Park Department.*"

Next I find an article on the fact that Sartre had a smoking "problem." "He quit and I can't," Uncle has written on the side. "Does that make me a better philosopher?"

This is too close to me, to now, and I remember the hospital, the moan of pain as his organs, mostly his lungs, dropped out of service because of the cancer. Two weeks ago he had been shaving himself when I arrived, plowing the whiskers, thick and gray, like a field, carving out the hollows of his cheeks, bringing the freckles out, the Rotatract whirring. In the gauge, the bead of oxygen jiggled high. A splash of witch hazel on his cheeks, a draw of air, words, words to explain, just the final everlasting statements of what you are, what you should be.

I pull out 18889:00090, in the center of the room, halfway down in the stack, once a box for Hush Puppies, size 9½, a beagle slumping on the box.

336-676-9: a clip of a psychedelic painting by Peter Max, from a magazine, bordered in black Magic Marker.

336-656-9: a packet made from an index card taped around the edges. Inside: pot seeds, crushed to powder.

336-676-9: a note from Grandfather on company letterhead, the factory embossed large across the top, handwritten, large letters, "Check enclosed for train tickets. All of us excited to see you soon. Bring Justin along as we discussed. All love."

336-677-9: a photograph from *Life*, the new miniskirts, faded color, wrinkles along the sides where the paper has been folded and refolded into itself.

"You won't want to go through all that," Justin said regarding the stuff in my uncle's hotel room, not *the* library itself. "It's a scatalogical outpouring, a mania. When you see how much there is, you'll give up."

Each morning fog came off Puget Sound. The fog was important because it settled the mood over the city. Abnormally—so they told me—it cleared by late morning and we had good weather every afternoon those two weeks, bright blue December sky, the caps of mountains.

In the hospital bed, folded down slightly, he hunched over alone, moaning to himself, wading through painkillers and the pain itself, waves of it, the concave sound of his breathing, bubbling like pond muck.

Olive scarves of seaweed wrapped around the pylons of the Pike Place Market. I wandered the cold fish counters, piled high with chips of fresh ice and the red flanks of salmon. I spotted the man named Bill, Uncle's friend, big, huge, one whose gravitational pull I cannot evade, like a fat all-knowing detective on a television show. He chewed a toothpick and eyed me up and down before talking, and when he spoke, his words were selected one at a time; the wooden toy boats he makes floated in plastic tubs. We had little to say except how sorry we were, in the cant of the mourning, the babble of grief. For a moment we babbled together like two birds, standing on the warped ancient boards of the market. Then he gave me the key, the address, and wished me good luck and turned away.

Numbers to the left: fifth box down, third pile over from the wall, dusty, dried, the paper flaking from acid. I flick the numbers, no subject headings here, just numbers: 888-098-54, 888-099-67. Placing the box down on the floor, I pull some out; a packet with a piece of soft cotton rope, the kind he used to use as a belt; an insurance form from the merchant marine, which he joined after the war; packet 888-098-54 has an old condom, still foil wrapped, crisp as a cornflake; I pull the last clipping from the end of the second row, a poem from a 1951 *New Yorker* by someone named Gene Baro called "For Hani, Aged Five, That She Be Better Able to Distinguish a Villain." In black ballpoint the lines are underlined:

> and we are betwixt and between what is and what might
> have been. To get the facts of nefarious acts,
> we must be free of predilections, preconceptions, dis-
> proportions,
> and distortions; we must be various, vicarious.

The poem is marked 888-908-45.

About twenty boxes, Florsheim shoes, unmarked, make up the core of his library, the central two stacks.

I pull open these core boxes at random. Clipped apart, the pornography is plasticine, fluid, disjointed, three-by-four, cut-down-to-size organs, pink folds, packed tightly, box after box. His scissors have removed the flanks of lovers, the object of stimuli, the head attached to the body, or the body that went with the head. Cut to size for storage are lips out of context, swollen appendages caught midthrob in a flash, a mishmash of haunches and open legs.

The real desire is cut away. The only order I see lies in the sexual predilections of whatever year is being looked at, and even that is erratic, dependent on obscenity laws or what happened to come his way. Most things carry over year to year. Just as many men with men in 1969 as 1975.

033: lips, mouths, kisses   044: penises, alone

I find only two photographs saved in their entirety, folded to size, crackling apart along the creases when I open them. Two men, white as porcelain, scarred with pimples, holding each other dearly. In the second full-sized photo, an orgy is in full swing, tangled forearms, the real thing, it seems, their absorption with each other melts the lens away.

Flash cards of flesh, the words are lost to me.

I remember that pain is matter with form. In the hospital his legs were folded wrong, his gown slipped open and the ancient walnuts of his scrotum slipped out, no longer "private parts," less obscene than the rest of his body.

The body will be taken care of. No services are to be performed, or any kind of memorial, at least not here. When the Pacific Medical Center returns the ashes, they will be shipped to Ohio and buried in a small plot, amid the smell of onion grass and ragweeds, on a shadowy hill north of our town, next to Grandfather and the rest of the family.

Each shoe box is approximately eleven-and-a-half by six. One inch contains, I figure, approximately one hundred clips, fragments, bits of prose. I calculate around two thousand or so clippings per box, if not more; about five hundred shoe boxes in all, not including the storage unit in Chicago, a million clippings.

In box 76667:09888 I find some letters from Grandfather, clipped apart:

000-379-9: Dear Russell,
Lovely hearing your voice the other night. Your mother was as delighted as I was. Enclosed is a check. Buy yourself a new tie, a coat, for the trip out. Of course we'll be at the station to meet you. New York Central. December 20th. 6:15 P.M.

000-379-0: Dated August 5, 1959
Dear Russell,
Perhaps no one can overcome being disliked by

another human being, especially the brother of the one human being you truly love. I know I can't. Mister, that last trip out still rings in my ear like one of Poe's bells. If your brother weren't so fucking all-American, if only he didn't run around in those cable knit sweaters. And, please note: his bright hair isn't a genetic mutation, it's an affirmation of his own personality. That Christmas was beyond belief for the two of us. Bile comes to my mouth thinking about it. "For Jesus sake dad, he hasn't worked a day in his life, and he's a fucking fairy." Do we need that? Did we need that? I love you. I want you. I have this long desire to have what is mine again, to need you. Love, Justin.

What droll urgency numbers have by quantifying, by their own being, by their very existence.

After three hours, my only conclusion is that his letters often begin with the prefix 000.

Only with time can panic come to fruition: time, over need, like a fraction: time/need = panic. "We have all the time in the world," he liked to say, and he did, for a while.
Panic hits after a few hours of looking through the boxes. His brother would want to burn the library. His lover might like to keep a box and throw away the rest. Back in the Midwest, the rest of the family would nullify whatever is here with their grief.
"Could you blame me," Justin said. "I could only take so much and then I just threw up my arms and gave up. For the last five years I didn't see him, really, except on the street with his friend from the market, what's his name? He has a system, but I could never figure it out."

*   *   *

In box 76998:00909 I find mostly photos:

786-898-8: a sprig of honeysuckle from an ad, outlined in black marker.

676-909-9: the Gerber baby's face with a circle around it.

789-851-0: James Dean in the bean field in *East of Eden*.

988-987-7: a quote from a magazine, blocked out in marker:

Psalm 30: "Thou has turned my laments into dancing. Thou has stripped off my sackcloth and clothed me with joy."

780-978-0: A postcard of the Chicago YMCA, folded to size.

When the nurses are done and the floor is streaked from the mop, and the room is pure with the blue smell of fresh bleached linen and piss, I rub his temples and his forehead and kiss his face.

The oxygen is off, the tiny bead resting on the bottom of the tube. He shoves the Camel deep into the flame, a good half inch.

"Sartre could quit smoking. I couldn't. Does that make me a better philosopher?"

"Sure."

"I want you to meet Bill, down at the market," he says. "He'll have the key to my room, and you can do what you want with it as you see fit."

"But we have the key to your room."

"No. This is *the* room. Not the Coat of Arms Hotel."

The Coat of Arms, a vast baroque hulk, a wasteland of

deformed vets, of Purple Hearts, smelly half-dead winos. A front. A place to reunite with the family.

I turn away to find Demerol, to beg the nurse. I crank the oxygen to a high of five. The doctors nod into clipboards and give up; the cancer is everywhere. He's a goner. As he suffers, I move around the city with loads of tourist maps, taking buses, the monorail. After my visit to the market, the key is in my pocket.

Draw a conclusion. Obligations call us back. I yank boxes out from under each other, and the stacks tumble over. Panic pumps through me. It is raining outside, and the drops glance off the broken windows. The humid rank smell comes into the hazy room. The floor is sagging. My flight, I think, my flight, my flight.

Folded tight, a page from a story by Sherwood Anderson marked 555-999-09. And photos of my grandfather in front of the big house. A photo of my mother, blocked in black marker; a photo of Justin, his face young and tan, on a beach.

Is there a trick, or is this a trick? It is clear to me that the numbers were placed down as he went along, chronologically, and at random, at the same time orderly and without order. A pile tumbles over and I kick at the spill, slick magazine print, newsprint, flashes of glossy paper. I pile and swish the clippings, mashing it all down, kicking.

Before I go I pull the packet from the front of the most recent box, the one I saved for last, and read exactly what I expected to read, his final statements: Paul Tillich: "A real symbol points to an object that can never become an object." Thomas Merton: "Death contributes something decisive to the meaning of life."

Then, his own writing, "Whatever we have shared is above and beyond 'time.' That's enough for me! Sort of hope all possessions can be given away rather than sold.

Whatever's 'appropriate.' Whatever happens, do not let the following people examine the materials in this library:" The list was a long one and went on, alphabetized, for pages. There were many names I did not know, and many that I did know.

It falls to my imagination to produce a movie called *The Library of Desire*. The order of the images, of the clippings, does not matter because this is a deep and meaningful movie; it insists on its own seriousness. Uncle Russell's life is formed in montage. One shot is of a young man getting off the train and stepping into the hazy light of a midwestern afternoon, golden, fuzzed by filtered lens, the iron rails of the track waving heat, chrome gloss; the shot lifts up into the air and shows the depot, the streets crosshatched out from it, a coal yard with black piles. It is hot, hot, and the insects rule the soundtrack with their shrill calls. The shot pulls back a bit further and one can make out the large homes on the avenue, and, amid them, the largest house of all, dark green, a broad front porch; the camera begins to lower and move into the tar-speckled roof, the square yard. By the movement itself you know it is the home of the boy, his place in the land, his destination.

The final scene, after his death, is that of two men in the secret room dancing together over a sea of clippings, gently, under the androgynous light, the young man's chin just touching the forehead of the bereaved lover. The credits are rolling, the long list of gaffers and sound men. The camera is swooping low to pick up the edge of crumbling files, clippings, a torso, a poem called "Blue Ice."

The real camera swoops down on me in the last dramatic scene, the next morning, saying goodbye to a dying man. The script of his life calls for it. The morning light presses through the rain, and the mountains are consumed with fog. Justin drives me to the hospital, following the reflector nubs in the middle of the road. The key Bill gave me is in my pocket. I sit on the bed and watch the pain play with him, fold him up, turn him over, until I find a nurse to save him from it.

She comes with the potion, and I tell him it was on its way.

"Do you want some good drugs?"

The smile comes from the root of his neck.

The nurse counts to herself as she eases it in.

"I'll shave you while you're getting stoned," I say, snapping the black wedge of technology on and working the rotors over the gray.

I leave him in delirium, smelling like witch hazel.

I sit looking through the scratched window. I pretend the audience is standing by their seats, waiting out the roll call of caterers, complimentary hotels, stunt men, and medical advisors.

Now the plane lifts up. The movie is not over because I still want to be back there with him as he lives. But it's already too late because I'm off the ground, cutting into the nimbostratus, breaking out over the flat skillet of sky into the afternoon blaze of sun tucked in the sky. At that moment, I am saved. Mount Rainier pounds beyond the clouds into the air and drives into the blue, the snow crusting down her sides and the tip poking the sun.

The steward hands me the plastic headphones, sealed in a bag. I plug my mind in. A movie is beginning for our in-flight entertainment. An old rerun of I Love Lucy, the bongos pounding out the theme song—a film in a film, I think. It's one I've seen a million times. Ricky and Fred argue that being housewives is pretty easy stuff. A fight ensues. Lucy and Ethel take up employment at a candy factory while the two men attempt to iron, burn a shirt, pressure cook a chicken until it ends up on the ceiling. Lucy is stuffing her mouth with truffles when it occurs to me that Uncle Russell was in his prime when the show came out, a sleek, confused boy breaking out into a world where changing any kind of role was a bad joke.

The live audience is shrill and relentless, understanding the truth. All four look foolish and stupid in their new roles. By the end of the show, the universe is back to normal, but my uncle, in truth, is still alive.

The audience is stunned. The final scene is that of Russell's death in the twilight. As the last bits of Demerol smother the sense out of him, he breaks through the surface using his final reserves of energy to speak to his old lover, the best friend he ever had.

"The secret to my files is to look at every single thing carefully," he says.

The final words on the screen are: "Thanks to the City of Seattle."

The library of desire is closed. I swallow the key with my life. I let the City of Seattle tend to the building, the renovation, the destruction. The key stays in my stomach, or intestine, someplace down in my gut. When I die, they'll find it there, untarnished, smooth, cold, ready to open the missing door.

At
Point
Lookout

As they drove in silence back from the beach, over the coastal bridges, over the small clumps of blue-green razor grass and the ruffled white dune, onto the blatant gush of the Grand Central Parkway roaring smog-covered into the heart of Queens, they were all freshly burned, chilled in the hot air and very tired.

Trudy took the whole backseat lying down with her feet propped up on Gena's headrest and a towel wrapped around her face.

Danny was driving and shivering, breaking into wells of gooseflesh as the air pumped from the vents. He was concentrating too hard to reach down and close them. The traffic was hell, with plenty of half-drunk Jersey kids swaying home, weaving the lanes erratically.

Danny was thinking. He was thinking about Trudy in the backseat and his wife, Gena, sleeping next to him with her shoulder strap around her elbow so it wouldn't rub into her burn and her head against the upper edge of the rolled-down window. Her face was a ripe peach, pink around the edges, and grew redder toward the center until it became brilliant red, a nucleus of heat on her nose.

Danny was thinking very hard about the day they had just had and the things that it had just concluded. He imagined that his version of the story, of the way the whole summer had turned in on itself and finally come to an end on this one day, was probably as right or wrong as any other version: a complex summer of friendship and moral questioning had meted out, resolved itself into a conclusion that could be held in the mind and rotated, a perfect specimen—but of what?

He knew he had been judgmental in a smug way, prudish even, about Trudy. But he had felt some kind of loosening ground beneath him that summer, and now, at the end of the season, with a beach day behind them, he felt he finally understood what had happened.

Gena and Danny were married—a year ago—during a particularly warm November day, in in the cool, dark back-chapel of Riverside Church on the Upper West Side of Manhattan. Trudy, who was living in Chicago at the time working for a middle western public relations firm, had not attended the wedding, and as a result seldom regarded them now as a married couple, really; rather, they were simply a happy-go-lucky couple of friends who happened to be married. But her friendship with them seemed stronger as a result.

*   *   *

Driving up Broadway, Danny remembered the way Trudy told him the news in late June during lunch at the Café Armstrong in midtown, spilling it carefully in small increments, surrounded by wicker chairs, polished brass rails, mahogany paneling, and men with short, moussed hair wearing paisley ties.

"So I'm on the jitney with my Walkman on, and this man sits next to me, so of course I ignore him while he stares."

"Of course."

"Then after a while he asks me what I'm reading—even though the music's on loud and I can't hear him anyway. So all I see are these wonderfully sensitive, moving, delicious, full lips, and this gorgeous face with a twist."

"Twist?"

"Yeah, sensitive, kind of ruddy and extremely middle eastern looking, very olive and looking directly at me as he talked."

Danny stuffed Brie and Virginia ham on rye toast into his mouth and sipped from his very cold white wine while Trudy filled in the details. He was in the sheet-metal business, a contracting firm, mostly large building projects, and he made a lot of money at it. Trudy was impressed most by his combat experience in the Six-Day War, which he described to her teary-eyed and in a ragged, choked voice that was, to Trudy, poetically tinged with the agonies of a young Israeli man's moral and religious choices. She described his story, riding a helicopter above the Sinai desert and seeing it spread out like a burlap bag enveloping the dead in its folds.

Having never seen war, of course, Danny listened skeptically to her as he sipped his wine and nodded occasionally in affirmation.

"Are you sure he was in this war? I mean they're cele-
brating the anniversary and everything. It might be bullshit."

"Oh yeah, I'm sure."

"How?"

"Oh, he knows the details, Danny. All of them, his de-
scriptions of the Sinai are exact, right down to the fauna—
what little there is, and his stories are so vivid, intense."

After they kissed and hugged goodbye on the sidewalk,
Danny started down 28th Street to his office on Madison.
Taking in Trudy's story, he was confused and jealous without knowing exactly why, except maybe for the fact that he
had never fought in a war. He felt this might indicate some
lack in his own manhood: this war thing, which seemed
such a major attraction of Trudy's new lover.

The streets were crowded, and the heat, at midsummer,
was oppressive with the stench of rotting food, pretzels,
lamb shish kebabs grating on the corner. An old luxury hotel
had been converted to homeless housing, and they con-
gregated in front over the marquee staring at him blankly as
he strode past. From the windows, rags, towels, jeans,
shirts, and sheets fluttered all the way up the Georgian fa-
cade, sending colorful signals to the gods to come down, to
save somebody, to draw this useless ship out of the muddy
saltflats of mid-Manhattan.

Late in the summer Trudy called Gena on a Saturday
afternoon with the suggestion of a Sunday at the beach on
Long Island.

"Gena, can I ask one thing though?" she whispered
over the phone, her voice cracking slightly and sounding
staticky.

"Sure Trud, what is it?"

"Can we just stay off *the* subject."

"Yeah, why not, we'll steer clear of him if we can."

Whenever she mentioned Mr. X Trudy's voice became delicate, as if he were a fine sheet of Japanese paper, translucent, light, fragile and yet running at length with long wood fibers and really quite strong. *The* subject had been the subject for the whole summer, weaving through their conversations and meetings together and dominating Trudy's summer both psychologically and physically.

Their friendship had been distorted by the man who had introduced himself to Trudy on the Long Island Expressway in June; now, almost Labor Day, a fateful moment of decision was at hand for their friend.

Mr. X was putting his cards on the table. No debate, no more thinking it out; he would give up his wife, his family (two sons, one five, one eight), one of his Westchester houses and, probably, the Hamptons home and half of his sheet-metal fortune, for her—simple as that.

Trudy needed a day on the beach to sprawl in the sun and to decide. It was a very simple decision.

Trudy saw it as typical, classic even in that it involved pleasure, pain, greed, and a desire to do what was good and right. Gena and Danny on the other hand saw nothing classic about it at all. They just looked forward to some resolution, to the end.

"Like I said," reassured Gena on the phone, "we'll just remove him from the day, completely."

"Oh it'll come up, inevitably, and we'll get all intense about it, and Danny—as usual—will make all kinds of sarcastic comments about him and then we'll have a horrible time."

"No, I'll keep him under wraps, even he knows when it's time to shut up most of the time."

Gena watched Danny stretch out on the futon in the living room reading, his long, freckled legs curled over each other. He had been working his way through the biography of a war photographer who had photographed every single major war—WWI, Spain, China, and WWII, then Korea—before finally being killed by a land mine during the French stages of Vietnam. His last shots, hastily developed, showed that his lens had captured, frame by frame, his boots as they tilted skyward and were surrounded by the intricate leaves of various tropical ferns fuzzing green, then a final scruff of mud. Finding out that this hero of modern photography had died stepping on a swamp mine early in a meaningless war, after he had slogged in the ice-cold waters of a Normandy beach for four hours, and hidden out behind a burned-out landing vehicle snapping award-winning black-and-whites, seemed like bitter fate to Danny, not to mention a just punishment for having skipped to the end of the book.

They did not mention Mr. X on the drive to the shore; they even waited carefully until Trudy was down at the other end of the beach before they talked about it.

Gena slapped her *Times* down. "God." She sighed. "She's so fucking remorseful about this decision she has to make, and at the same time she's gloating about it."

"Gloating? I think it's called suffering."

"No, I mean I can feel this, as a woman, this kind of silence saying, 'I have to make this decision and *you* don't.'"

"Ah come on, Gena, you're overreacting—I think. I mean this is one of those life decisions everybody's talking about today. I mean sure, maybe she shouldn't be beating it with a stick like this. Maybe she should just be saying, Okay, I'll keep screwing the hell out of him and not make a commitment; he'll buy that, most men would."

Gena looked out at the gray water, at the men on the rocks casting lazily into the water. "Maybe the fact that we care so much about this reveals more about us than anything else. Why should we care? Why do we care?"

"We care for all the right reasons, because she's a friend. And, sure, we're married, and have taken a public stance on the issue by being so—even if people get married for many different reasons, it's still a kind of political statement about the world."

Danny closed his eyes. The sun had burned through a morning layer of high clouds and was beginning to intensify. He saw the red blood behind his eyelids. Mr. X marched toward him in olive combat fatigues on a heat wave-covered desert; his face was rutted, scarred, and his large brown eyes were wide, searching, asking why and crinkling up slightly in the corners. And then, Danny imagined, he opened his mouth wide, teeth pearly, glimmering, and his mouth began to suck up the heat and sunlight like a black hole. This was a man to be reckoned with, Danny told himself.

"I just wish we could talk to her, make her realize that it's going to fall apart in the long run. You can't support somebody with that much guilt in their past, can you, a whole backlog of pain?" Danny said.

"But we can't lecture her on it. It's a violation of her friendship, our intimacy. We're here to support, not to question her or to make her realize her future."

"But really good friendship is always a violation of intimacy."

Trudy was walking back down the beach toward them, looking out across the tiny niche of bay to the other side, where a long cycle of Jones Beach curved into the sea; the sand there was crammed with beach-goers, just black specks in the distance.

She wondered how it was, over there, where the loud

radios were sending dulled rock and roll into the air and the men strutted around bumping into each other; the women lay oiled up and waiting. Walking, she could almost taste the wet, salty, late-night goodbye kisses that awaited the teenaged girls out there.

Each step seemed curved with loneliness, as her feet drew back and then, on coming forward, scraped into the wet sand. Her hair, down, gathered up the breeze and knotted around her shoulders and into her mouth. She stopped, brushed the strands from her mouth and looked across the bay to the beach.

Seeing Trudy walking alone down the beach, Danny watched her and felt selfishly happy to be married. There is a great, terrifying void that needs to be filled out there, he thought.

Gena watched her coming back and could not blame her anymore. No one held blame, really. Trudy was lonely and Mr. X came in to fill up that empty spot in her life. There were plenty of creepy men out there, but he sounded normal, just a man having a rough time with the family and needing someone.

Trudy plopped down on her towel without a word. Obviously they had been discussing her problem. It was clear in the glance that passed between them when she arrived.

"Want some oil?" Gena asked, putting a glob of the copper-colored stuff on her palm and rolling it onto her own shoulder.

"Yeah, sure," Trudy said, holding her hand out. "Just a little bit, this stuff always drives me crazy, it's so oily."

"Where did you go?" Danny muffled, facedown on the towel.

"Just down to the changing rooms. They checked my ID tag, the old lady in the little booth shouted at me. 'Lady, madam, could I see your identification tag immediately.'

Quite an old bird, hunched over with a big wide hat and little round specs."

They laughed softly. For an hour they sat and lay in the sun. Danny read his biography of the war photographer, trying to imagine what it might be like to huddle out in the bitter cold Atlantic while tracer bullets flashed and buzzed past you, your legs numb, purple from the cold, feeling like they're going to fall off. Husks of dead men floated past you and all the while you were just trying in desperation to keep the lens free of water and spots.

Danny couldn't pin why he wanted to know about this man who had enmeshed himself in war and amid stupid death. He thought wars were stupid creations of the male ego system. But on the beach, with the summer beating down on New York City only thirty miles behind them, it seemed appropriate to be reading about survival in war.

Gena closed her eyes and concentrated on the purplish backs of her eyelids until everything went away and she was dreaming lightly about fish and water.

Meanwhile, Trudy thought about Mr. X, his rich eyes and the way his lips curved inward slightly when he smiled, bringing his cheeks out but not dimpling them ridiculously the way some men's did. She thought about his loving words, which were always softly spoken and never in that indirect way American men had; he looked right at you, never glancing away, full of the devoted concentration a biologist might have staring through his microscope. He had a certain amount of pent-up rage which would probably never escape but instead would power him, drive him. Trudy told herself—this was necessary, the world needed Mr. X and his power. It was worth the risk. But the decision. The decision.

It was past two o'clock and Danny was hungry so he went off and bought some franks at a stand and three sugar-free ice teas and some Cape Cod chips. When he returned both girls were sleeping soundly facedown in the sand.

After they ate, and waited the prescribed half-hour to ward off cramps, Trudy stood up, blocking the sun from their bodies, and suggested a swim. Gena, half asleep, mumbled about the cold Atlantic, but Danny was ready for a swim, hopped up and pulled her along with him. It felt good to hold her arm and to be walking to the water with someone like Trudy, someone who gathered up the looks on the beach.

The water was cold but not unbearable. They waded up to their hips and let gooseflesh break out before finally, after a count of three, diving deep into the brackish water.

Both of them felt a sudden, incredible isolation. The sounds of the beach were gone. Danny dug his toes into the rocky bottom, pushed up as high as he could and dove again. Trudy followed. Underwater they touched palms and he blew out air making muffled giggle sounds. She broke out laughing and thrust to the surface. When he came up she was there, still laughing, calling him a jerk.

"What's so funny?" he asked.

"Just you," she said, "you just make me laugh."

"It's nice out here," he said, flapping his hands on the water.

"Calm and nice."

"Let's dive down again," she suggested.

Again they dove deep and touched palms, and in the murky dark he made the puffed-out face. She started laughing and he made a low-pitched groan with bubbles and they both shot to the top.

Trudy squinted at the shore. "Is she asleep?"

"Probably," he said. "All she does on the beach is sleep."

"Let's swim out," she said. "Out to that thing out there."

She tossed herself up and began a quick crawl out to a sea buoy marking the outer reaches of the lifeguard area. Hesitating, Danny watched her then followed, doing a distorted version of the sidestroke that he had learned at the Y as a kid.

Was it simply the deception of the sea, which was unusually calm that day, or the surprising weakness of his arms that made it seem like such a long way out to the buoy, Danny wondered as he cupped his hands and curled each stroke, reverting to his clumsy crawl now to gain on Trudy. But it was far out and the current pulled hard.

Trudy reached the buoy and held on with one hand. It was flaking a crust of barnacles, peeled paint and rust.

When he finally reached Trudy, and clung onto the bobbing buoy, Danny was exhausted and breathing hard.

"Shit, that's far."

"It's not that far," she teased him.

"Not to you, Ms. goddamn champion swimmer of Orange County or whatever you were, shit, it's miles to me."

Danny watched a smile spread across Trudy's face. They were far from shore with a large span of gray water between themselves and the sand and those on it; there was a sense of depth that came from clutching onto a hulk of metal tethered to the sea floor by twenty feet of chain. Surrounded by cold Atlantic water they brushed toes.

They held the silence between them; Mr. X was gone, washed away by the taste of sea salt. The gulls lifted, expecting something from the land.

"I'm sorry I brought you guys into this whole mess," Trudy whispered. "That you should have to help me make such a personal decision is wrong, I think—and I know it was especially hard for you to deal with."

"Why me?" he asked, wondering how she could possibly know how the whole situation had thrown him off for weeks.

"I just figured that you were attracted to me at some level and that you were a little jealous about it somehow."

"Did it show, really?" he said, his voice sarcastic.

"Only when you joked about penis length."

They laughed.

"I didn't joke about him, not really. I thought it was an issue or something."

"Well, I've decided and I'm going to tell him that I can't see him again and that it's off. So, I'll be lonely, like here, just kind of bobbing around for a while in the gray—at least I'll be honest with myself."

"It's lonely out here but you know you can always swim in."

"Unlike you, you hardly made it out here."

Their ankles touched. "Yeah, Danny, it is like being out sometimes in the city, when you just sort of float and watch and nobody knows what you're doing or what you did. Shit, when we slept together, he and I, not a damn person ever knew, never; the old tree in the woods . . . no one heard it fall."

"Like us here, right?" He felt cheap immediately for saying it, but nervous about the proximity of her mouth as they held on together.

"Right, you could just kiss me and no one would know, care, or even think about the possibility."

He kissed her very gently and she returned the kiss, salty. Her arm reached around behind him and held the small of his back and for a moment they were suspended that way. Then, slowly, they kissed once more and held it while the water dripped from their faces. Danny felt the water shift a bit and pushed his body against her; there was a strong musty taste for both of them. It felt like the roaring wind in a shell, fumbling, falling backward like the tree in the woods thumping into the humus, exploding dust and pine needles into the air. Then, it was over and she pushed off toward shore silently, dipping her smooth stroke gracefully into the water's surface.

By the time they reached shallow water, Gena had walked to the shore and was wading in to join them. They splashed and played in the water, all three of them, pushing each other around, making gurgles and buzzing motorboat sounds, diving to the bottom and pulling up stones.

Weeks later when the whole day at the beach was only a dry sunburned memory, Danny read an article in the *Times* about the nuclear buildup and the increased dangers of impending war; it seemed to him a tired old cliche, like the Mr. X question—and yet it was, he knew, still there, still probably hanging over some portion of her life. So somehow, it didn't shock him so much when he spotted Trudy having lunch in the Café Armstrong, sitting in the front window with a middle-aged, well-dressed man. He was a good-looking man, Danny thought, watching his lips move silently through the glass, saying aggressively words he would never hear. Words that might bring an end to all this questioning.

A
Matter
of
Direction

A full moon begins to edge up as we hike our favorite trail, one that runs north from the house, across the frozen furrows of the garden, over a field covered with tight rows of saplings barely poking through the snow. We planted those trees last summer, pulled them from the back of a station wagon, took the burlap bags off the roots, sliced a hole in the soil with a shovel tip, and shoved them in. Hundred of them. For a whole day, we planted.

While we hike, I think about my sister, Kate. The thoughts are sparked by the way Jed tosses himself head-long in front of me. I figure if she were along, she'd be running too. She'd be excited by the possibilities, rushing into the sharp horizon of snow, to tear apart that perfect whiteness. She'd pull us both toward that spot on the earth where wrongdoing came up naturally like a hot, steaming spring.

My best friend Jed knows all about her. But tonight, even thinking about her around him makes me ashamed. He's heard about the time she stole a car with some friends, and her reputation in school for being easy, sexually I mean.

It's in her genes, I like to say, wondering, in the back of my head, if it's in *my* genes. As a joke to myself, I sometimes picture a pair of faded old jeans being passed from generation to generation. It's a lot of work justifying my own sister's wicked behavior. I excuse it as just another part of the universe, a distant solar flare that is picked up by a telescope but really happened a billion years ago.

We arrive above a slight gully made by the Penn Central railroad track to Chicago. By packing the snow with our boots, we make a level place on the hillside where we can wait, smoke, sip beers and watch the moon come up.

We sit down in the snow. I dig the pipe and tobacco out from the gunny sack.

"Try this," Jed says, handing me a silver pipe tool. It has a round blunt end to pack the tobacco. I take a wad of the sticky tobacco between my fingers and use my thumb to push it into the bowl.

"Pack that looser on the bottom then work it tight on top. My old man told me that."

I pack the bowl. The match flairs up. I draw the flame in and let the sweet smoke fill my mouth: it connects me to everything—the rusty taste of the plastic, chewed-up stem, the smell of snow mold.

I lean back in the snow. With the brim of my hat down

over my eyebrows, I release a huge puff of smoke into the air.

"Won't be long," Jed says in a whispery, excited voice. He nods for my pipe, takes a suck, gurgles a drink of his Bud. Then, with his hand to his forehead, he looks down the tracks.

"Let's get the slingshots out," he says.

"Yeah, sure, why not."

The type of slingshots we're using are illegal, by rule of the city council. They have a bracket that comes around the bottom of your arm to give you leverage when you pull the thick tube back. Hunters use them. Some kid killed his brother with one.

Jed opens a bag of corn chips. He's eating them like an anteater, picking the yellow chips off his palm with his tongue.

I haven't told Jed that my sister isn't at home anymore, that she's in the hospital. He'd be intrigued, and I'd have to describe the old brick hospital building, half renovated with new, mirrored-glass windows and indoor-outdoor nylon carpet the color of rotted pumpkin in the hallways. Jed would pry the whole sordid tale out of me; how she locked herself in the bathroom all day when she found out she was going, crying to herself until Dad got a hacksaw from the basement and began to saw at the doorknob; how Dad and I hauled her to the hospital on Wednesday night, right when the blizzard was beginning. From there the story would disintegrate into a kind of violent asylum melodrama. Jed would love that part.

To kill time, Jed makes a few snowballs, packs them so hard that they squeak, and then whips them into the gully, one by one.

"She's real late," he mentions, pulling his cap off for

what must be the hundredth time, scraping at his hair with his fingernails.

The tracks below shine wet and slick in the light from the moon. They are busy rails, glossed frequently by trains. I love what they are to me: two hunks of metal laid across the land all the way to Chicago, or Detroit, depending on the way you go.

Jed gives his luminous watch dial a good, long stare.

"Do we have enough ammo?" I ask him.

Out of his coat pocket he pulls a plastic bag filled with lead pellets.

"How's this?" Like a comet, the bag sighs through the air before I catch it and finger the weights, heavy and soft.

"She must be running late," he says again. "It takes what, five, ten minutes from the time she leaves the station until she gets here?"

He sticks a pellet into the leather pouch of his slingshot, lies back into the snow; I do the same, looking up into flurries that have just begun falling. There are only a few clouds. The snow seems to come from nowhere.

The pellet zings into the moonlight. We listen silently for a moment to the soft whisper of snow hitting snow.

Then we hear a low hum far away, over the snow, the distant creak of tension in the rails. All of a sudden my heart's a big punching bag swinging in the center of my brain.

"She's coming," Jed says, delighted.

I slip four of the weights into the front corner of my coat pocket.

From the east the diesel sound increases.

Jed stands, perfectly still, a few yards to my right, crouching down a little at his knees, whispering, "Yeah-oooo, I'm gonna blast her to Chicago."

The huge beam from the headlamp glances off the

snow, around the curve, and into our eyes. When it makes the bend we see a square-headed diesel—a freight pusher, really—painted red, white and blue, but showing gray and white in the moonlight.

Before we can think, it swings into the right-of-way, a snake of ribbed cars, all glistening chrome, faces in the small windows, looking out.

Jed shoots first. A small flower of orange spark blooms off one of the cars.

"That was it," he screams, loading up for another one. "Shoot."

I pull back as hard as I can until the long rubber tube is to my ear and both my arms are shaking. I don't want to let go, but when I see the engine centered in the Y, I hold my breath to steady my arm, aim, then release the pouch.

For a split second—for no reason at all—I imagine that somewhere on the land, alone in a field of snow, a deer is nosing a salt lick, unaware; elsewhere, at the bottom of the pond next to Jed's house, fish wade the deepest reaches of the muck.

With the sound of old, dried wood being pried apart, the train brakes to a stop.

A metallic taste flows in my mouth as if I've swallowed a mouthful of nickels. Beneath me, my legs go loose.

Jed rocks back and forth, his weapon at his side, limp in his hand, his mouth wide open.

The train has stopped dead, seven passenger cars behind the engine, and all along the row of tiny windows— ablaze with light—are faces looking out, searching the woods for us.

"Back," Jed chokes.

Stumbling and slogging through the snow, we retreat as fast as we can, along the edge of the gully and then back into a clump of woods. Panting like a couple of dogs, we lift our knees high against the snow.

"Are there two faces in that cab?"

Jed squints. "Yeah. They probably think something broke off the track and flew up under the train or something."

"This was stupid," I say to him, softly, shoulder to shoulder, hunched down against a pine trunk that is sticky with white frozen sap. Pine needles mat a dry ring around the base of the trunk, crunch under our boots.

Jed's teeth chatter. He reaches up to adjust his hat, carefully.

"Somebody's coming out," I say. A man clambers down the ladder, slowly, a zero-gravity descent to the moon. His flashlight lasers around the air. He pokes the beam of light under the engine, at the huge wheels and the tracks. Then he sways it out and around the woods.

The slice of light comes over the pine needles and hits the trees around us, making them suddenly alive and brown and real. Then it's gone, sweeping further down, bringing out more trees before fading.

When we have the courage to look out again, the man is climbing back into the engine.

The train gushes white steam along the full length of its wheels, and then pulls out, slowly. Picking up speed, we hear it moving toward Chicago, blasting its horn, already far, far away.

"Yeah-oooo." Jed slaps his glove on my back and fluffs a stinging scoop of snow into my face. "That sucker was pissed. That engineer probably thought he hit a deer or something."

"Next time I'm gonna knock the damn headlight off the thing," he tells me, making chopping motions with his arms, demonstrating his future ability to use martial arts against a fifteen-car train. "Ha ya, ha ya, ha ya," he shouts with each chop.

We take a different way back to the house, around the pond Jed's dad made himself with a state water grant. I carry the gunny sack and keep my mouth shut. There's nothing to say.

"Well, we did it," he says to me in his driveway. A big smirking grin covers his whole face and seems to lift his hat up a few inches on his scalp.

"Did what?"

"We did it!"

"What did we do?"

He kicks the driveway with his boot, shrugs, then looks up at the sky like the answer's there.

"Sure snowin' hard again."

"Yeah, well."

"Maybe come out next weekend. I'll have the ice cleared. Dad fixed the snow blower. We can skate."

"Sure."

I drive straight from Jed's house to the hospital. The roads are slick and icy. Only the plows are out, flicking rock salt from their rumps.

A few lights are on in the building. In the darkness, I can see into the nursing stations where all night the nurses smoke, drink coffee from Styrofoam cups, and read tabloid stories of the miraculous.

I ring the buzzer and a bulky nurse arrives behind the sliding doors, her uniform as tight as an ace bandage across her bosom.

She unlocks the door and shoves it open a crack.

"Visiting hours are over," she says. She looks tired. Mascara has flaked over her eyes, and her lipstick is gone in the spot where her cigarette rested.

"I have to see my sister," I plead, desperation in my voice. It's real. I must see her.

She asks my name. I give it to her. She knows the name. Her daughter is in school with me, a fat, unpopular girl I've never talked to before. But there is a connection between us. In the doorway the nurse smiles; she's my savior tonight. Behind me I feel the cold, dark weight of a winter night.

"She's on the second floor, room two-twenty, take the stairs, second door to the right," she whispers, putting her finger to her lips.

Except for the sigh of air dragged through ducts, the long hallway is silent.

I knock softly on her door.

There's a stirring of sheets being tossed back from a bed; the door opens, and she is there in her long, white nightgown, her hair back in a ponytail, the room dark behind her.

"Rudy?" she whispers in a voice that seems pumped full of air.

"I had to see you."

"How'd you get in this place? It's past eleven isn't it?"

"Alice Harper's mother let me in."

Inside the stuffy room there is just enough light to see her bed, as small as a foldaway cot, shoved up against the wall. Another door, to my right, is open; inside I see a mirror glinting over a sink. Dominating the room is a large window looking out the back of the building: a scraggly vacant field cut by Potowit Creek, which was named for the Indians who settled the valley.

"Nice view," I tell her, sweeping my arms out as if to grab it all and bring it inside. I'm not sure if it's that nice. Gritty, dank, and alive, marsh weeds poke through the snow. Water moves in the moonlight where the ice hasn't seized the river.

"Sure, not bad for the funny farm," she says.

She sits down on the bed. "What are you here for?" she says, abruptly.

"I was thinking of you out at Jed's house, and on the way back I thought it would be good to see you—"

"In this snow? Why now, Rudy?"

"I don't know," I say, honestly, feeling a sinking feeling in my gut, as if I'd been tossed from a cliff.

"They drugged me you know, that's why I'm calm—I think."

"I know that." Her voice has regained a calm, trusting tone, and I understand that she is just glad to have me there in that lonely room while the snow is falling outside. In her white gown, she is like a ghost; and her lowered voice is utterly unreal as it slides through the room.

It feels good to be with her in the darkness where our eyes cannot meet and make that commitment that sight brings: where our disembodied voices seem to rise into the warmed air.

"I came here to tell you something, I think."

"Yeah?"

She stands beside me where we can look out the window at the scene below.

"At Jed's we fell into a little trouble."

"What kind of trouble did you fall into?"

"We shot a train with our slingshots. And the train stopped, right there in the middle of the field. It just stopped while the engineer got out and checked the engine." She's listening. I can feel it. "I feel bad about it. But I couldn't stop myself because Jed was hanging over me and—well— you know that Jed never was one for not finding trouble if it's around."

Her breath reaches me and smells medicinal—of sulfur and rust.

"You don't fall into trouble, Rudy," she says to me. "Trouble comes when something wrong seems right."

We are both looking out at the creek, at the way it hooks around into a tight *U,* forced that way by some underground feature of the geology.

"But if they didn't see you, I wouldn't worry too much," she says in a voice that is miles and miles away.

"What the world doesn't see or hear or know you can't worry about. You can't. The things people *do* see, the things they do notice, are enough. Anyway, *you* know how you feel about it and that's what matters."

"Yeah, I guess I do."

"You must forgive yourself. They say that's my first step, to forgive myself. And then, if I'm lucky, other people in my life will forgive me."

"That seems simple enough."

"It sounds simple, but it's not. It sounds like one of those posters you see in the card stores, with a cat hanging from a tree branch, that say 'hang in there.' But in this case, it does seem to be true."

A wedge of light from the hallway fills the room. Gently, the nurse says it's time for me to leave and then the door shuts and we're alone again.

My sister lets out a small gasp and begins to cry. Holding her is like holding a frail butterfly wing melting beneath your fingers. She's light and hollow-boned like a bird. It fills me with the memory of a time when hugging and walking with my arm over her shoulder were natural. I let her cry in my arms. Outside, flurries of wind pick snow up into the air across the field that reaches, eventually, all the way to the shore of Lake Michigan. There the waves are coming in on mounds of ice, adding to them with each crash, until they become so huge that you can't see beyond them to the water.

"You're going to come out right," I tell her, for the first time believing that in many ways she would.

"You too." She sniffs. And we both laugh.

It's in her genes, I think as I'm driving home. And then I think: It just doesn't matter. There will be plenty of things I don't understand, things that I will do and regret long after they're over, things that will take a long time to forgive.

McGregor's
Day
On

McGregor walked to work each day pondering the high psychic cost of his own success. He considered himself more a philosopher than a businessman; more a thinker than a doer. But despite his philosophical bent, he still wore a suit to work each day.

It was late October. The dank stench of summer air had been shoved aside by a succession of Canadian cold fronts. The air was clear. McGregor drew deep breaths with each few steps. It felt good to take in as much air as possible. On the West Side, where he lived with his wife, the trees in Riverside Park had exploded into color one weekend, and then, just as quickly, dropped their leaves. Now the scrawny elms in front of the brownstones were whisked clean. Although the world was dying, McGregor felt a brisk, invigorating sense of transformation, which seemed for the good.

Inside the elevator he wedged himself between two men from the real estate firm on the fourteenth floor. He knew their faces from previous trips. Behind him, there was the brooding silence of people on their way to work. He faced his own fuzzy reflection in the silver doors. Even in the scratched metal, his sharp chin showed; his thick black eyebrows; the scoop of his receding hair. When the elevator jerked to the first stop and the doors slid open, he was startled. His body split in two. As he stepped aside to let the men through, one tossed him a nervous glance. The doors slid shut again. He ignored his own reflection, or tried to, looking at the numbers light up.

He was startled again when he reached his floor. The doors opened and Harrison Blake was standing outside facing him. He wore a white shirt, the collar of which pressed into his neck. His dark black skin was almost purple in the dim light and against the white walls of the lobby.

"Oh," Blake said when their eyes met. "Oh, I'm going up."

McGregor held the door open. It jerked against his hand, pulled back, then tried to shut again. Someone in the elevator said, "Come on, let it go or get on."

But Blake's voice had made McGregor pause. He waited for Blake to say more.

"I'm going up to personnel to see Jacobson," he said.

McGregor got out and let the door slide shut.

"Sorry," he said, "but I couldn't hold it any longer."

"That's all right," Blake said, his voice even softer. It seemed to fade into the noise of the building, the clicking of elevator cables behind the doors. "I'm in no hurry, actually."

"You're either getting fired or going over the new dental plan," McGregor said. "Or both."

"Right," Blake said and punched the up button. "I'm getting fired account of deese teeth," he said, parting his lips into a mock smile. "They be too white. Too white for the likes of you."

They were bright, perfect teeth, McGregor noticed; it felt strange to look at his teeth that way, to really look closely at them.

Blake closed his lips and didn't smile.

"You're a wit on wheels," McGregor said, smiling hard at Blake. "The funny man." His jaw ached. It had been a long time since they had laughed together at anything.

"Lighten up McGregor," Blake said. Then he let a genuine smile break over his face. "God knows I can't lighten up." He held up the back of his arm to the light and examined it closely.

"Blake," McGregor said. "Seriously, Blake. Maybe it's time we sat down and talked this out a bit. I mean, I don't know what Jacobson's deal is. I hear things. But maybe I can help out in some way. And, anyway, it's been a long time since—well, since, you know. Okay?"

"I'll let you know."

When the elevator doors closed on Blake, the cables clanked and sang in the long shafts, running all the way up to the thirtieth floor and down into the deep recesses of the basement. In his mind, McGregor saw Blake being hauled up through space and time by the big drum-wrapped cables, away and outward.

"I've got to get to work," he said in the building's stuffy air.

By ten o'clock, McGregor was engulfed by several projects: a contract for a Japanese edition of an American children's book on barn owls, an easy sale of a German title to an American publisher, a fax sent to a subagent in Spain, a

friend who wanted McGregor to represent his book of stories, a first serial deal to a magazine, and another friend who
wanted to plan a weekend ski trip to Vermont. Under this
load, he became so involved that he took no notice when
Blake returned to his office.

McGregor continued to work, typing and sending more
faxes to England, Japan, and West Germany, feeding the
sheets one at a time into the machine and listening to it beep
and dial: A green light spread across the paper as it fed,
seeping out from the underside of the machine—a magic
luminous fluid that picked the print from the page and piped
it a few thousand miles away. Speed and magic, McGregor
thought, typing a Telex to a Madrid newspaper.

At lunchtime, Blake appeared in McGregor's doorway
with his arms up on the doorjambs and his overcoat on.

"You've been busting your chops today," Blake said.
He looked behind McGregor out the window where the sky
was gray, mottled and dirty; and the wind was blowing so
hard the glass flexed and shook.

"Too many deals," McGregor said, immediately wanting to take it back. "How was it with Jacobson?"

"It was," he answered. "Jacobson has his job; I have
mine." Then he shrugged and let go of the door frame.

"Anything I should know about?"

"I'm not sure," Blake said. "To be perfectly honest—
well, not perfectly, but at least a little bit honest, I'm not
sure if it's something anybody should know about or not."

Blake went to the window and put his palms to the cold
glass. "Questions," he said, his lips close to the glass, whit-
ening it with his air.

McGregor turned in his chair to face him and said,
"Let's simplify this thing."

"What thing?"

"Everything, today, right now. I don't know what's

bothering you, exactly, but maybe at least I can show you how to prioritize them."

"You would," Blake said as he sunk and squeaked back into the director's chair.

"What'dy mean by that?"

"You know sometimes you sound like one of those horrible self-help manuals you try to sell," Blake said. "You could prioritize your life into the ground if you had time. Lucky for you, you don't have the time—'cause you've got a whole load of priorities to prioritize, if you know what I mean."

"And not a lot of ground to prioritize them into," McGregor added.

Blake sat again, hanging his long leg over the wooden arm of the chair. It sagged under the weight. His pant cuffs slid up past his socks.

Then McGregor said, suddenly, "Let's take the rest of the day off and get out of this place."

"You mean shirk our responsibilities to the job at hand?" Blake put both legs over the arm of the chair. "Personnel would not like that."

"Maybe not," McGregor said. "But I wanted to prioritize; and, well, taking the afternoon off seems to be the first on the list—at least the first that is applicable to the two of us, equally."

The lobby floor was dark and glossy, freshly waxed. A delivery man stood by the check-in desk, leaning against his dolly. He eyed their silk ties; the almost-matching knee-length mohair coats, cuffed trousers breaking slightly over spit-polished oxfords, and watched them as they went through the revolving door, rubber seals gulping air.

On the street, afternoon shadows, big and blocky, fell across the sidewalks.

"We're free," McGregor said and spun around in two complete circles, his coat splaying out like a ballerina's tutu.

He faced Blake, whose expression revealed only annoyance at his friend's overdramatic gesture.

"Do you feel guilty—taking time away from the job?" McGregor said.

"No, not really," Blake said. But his voice sounded tight. He was lying. They were the pained words of a lie, McGregor thought.

Where did that pain come from? He knew so little about his friend. He had guessed that Blake was ashamed of his background, imagining some Deep South childhood of poverty, skimped meals, and the desertion of a father.

"Personnel might be down on me for taking off an afternoon, but I'm certainly not down on it," Blake said, stepping off. "Come on."

They took McGregor's usual route to the subway, down Twelfth Street, past Sixth to the Seventh Avenue entrance near St. Vincent's Hospital, where cars double-parked to pick up or drop off patients.

"Just as many people are coming out as going in," McGregor pointed out. "I notice that every day. The great equalizer, hospitals."

"If you're lucky they are. If you're not, you die."

"I'll think about that," McGregor said.

They sat silently on the train. They had failed to achieve the proper words, the necessary chitchat. McGregor did want to say something right, something that would get to the heart of the matter—if he knew what that matter really was. He wanted to ask Blake, 'Is silence the great equalizer? Did I break us apart?' He could barely recall the night their friendship had ended, when Blake had become unwilling to let the walls down. McGregor could only understand his own bitterness. It grew from his own opinion of himself as a compassionate man. I am a compassionate man, he told himself repeatedly. I am. It is the one thing about myself of which I am totally sure.

But with Blake he came up against something hard and unmoving.

It had happened one night, the previous spring, when a freak blizzard struck and the railroads were shut down because of the snow. Blake could not get north to his home in Westchester and his wife, Malona. The streets were clogged with the heavy flakes. When McGregor invited him to stay the night at his apartment, Blake hesitated and called the train station several times before saying yes. Even then, he did not sound enthusiastic about the idea. He said yes with a sigh, as if giving in.

That night, with the snow falling gently outside, they got drunk together in the jazz room at the West End bar, a gritty, beer-stained place on Broadway near Columbia. With the heat, the noise, and the music, they did little talking at first. But soon the ritual of drinking together, of lifting glasses in unison to their lips, matching vodka tonics one on one, made them want to talk.

"Blake, now that we're drunk, can I be honest with you?"

"You mean you aren't, usually?"

"That's funny. But what I mean is, can I be really honest with you?"

"I certainly hope so."

McGregor drank and wiped his mouth. "Blake, this is the Eighties, right? And my parents raised me to be open-minded about Blacks and to always respect them—but I never had any black friends, really. You're the first. So whatever I can know about black people, I'll know from you, to be honest. But you don't say much about who you are. Not really."

Blake pointed his finger to get the bartender's attention and ordered a whiskey straight up.

"To be blunt, fuck your parents, McGregor," he said, coughing after a swallow of his drink. "I don't want to shock you, but that's old ditty shit. My parents raised me to respect white people. What does that mean? You pull that one out of your vest pocket like a magic scarf, when the fact of the matter is you're scared of me the way I am. Why you want to know so much is because you're scared."

"I'm not scared to share with you, Blake. My life's an open book. My head's swimming I'm so drunk."

"Your life has been an open book since Plymouth fuckin' Rock." Blake held his glass near his chin and looked into the lineup of bottles behind the bar, backlit, glimmering.

"White people been shoving that open book in our faces since God knows when. And I'm not bitter. Don't get me wrong, McGregor. You wanted honesty, but don't get it wrong when you get it. This is the Eighties and you're getting the end-of-the-decade truth from me is all. And the truth is that nothing is as simple as digging up a few of a person's past facts and then thinking that fills out the whole story."

He swirled the ice in his drink. When they'd first arrived, the musicians had been working over a few sentimental, overblown pieces. The quartet had seemed so bored with the music that they were ready to fall off the rickety platform. As the night got deeper, though, the sets began to build. Now the men seemed uncontrolled, flaying away at the instruments.

"What do you want to know about me McGregor?" Blake said.

"What do I want to know?"

"Yes. What is it that I can tell you that would really make a difference between you and me?"

After he finished off the bottom of his drink, McGregor said, "I don't know. Let me think."

"How much time you need? You already had a couple of centuries. Down deep, you just know that any question you come up with will be an answer."

"You're drunk Blake."

The trumpet player was working his solo, drawing out the notes long and sorrowfully, as if pulling them out from the bell of his horn with a long rope. When he changed notes it was by pushing the keys down so slowly that they melded into each other.

"Does Jacobson treat you like the rest of us?"

"Who, him? In his fucking handmade shirt collars and deluxe wide striped seersucker with the French fly. No kidding. We were in the john pissing together and he tells me his tailor gives him a wide selection of zippers or whatnot for his flies. There he is giving me a history of his pants in earnest detail. Next thing, he calls me into his office to wonder why I'm not earning out this year's advance, and all I can do is try not to look at his crotch, wondering what kind of latch he's got between the world and his underwear."

"Don't make me laugh. That man has our lives in his hands."

"Ain't that the truth."

The crowd was getting silent. The trumpet player persisted taking all the air from the room.

"I don't know what to say," McGregor whispered.

"That's the point," Blake whispered back.

As the audience began to applaud McGregor saw his friend's lips set firmly together in an embouchure, as if he were finishing the trumpet solo.

The music ended. "Let's go," Blake said. "It ain't gonna get better or worse than that solo."

They went out onto snow-covered Broadway, staggering drunk. So clear and fresh, it wasn't any city they knew; it was like Bedford Falls in *It's a Wonderful Life*. Cars were stopped dead in the street, abandoned and left on their own. In the wedge of gray sky between the buildings, McGregor could trace the paths of flakes high into the sky.

"God am I drunk," he said.

"I'm not too bad."

"You're as drunk as I am, at least."

"How the hell do you know that?"

McGregor put his arm around Blake's shoulder, "Because we matched each other glass for glass and you can hardly walk now—and don't blame the snow for the way you walk. You're as good as drunk and you know it." He squeezed Blake against him.

Blake twisted out from under his arm. "Get the fuck off me," his voice cracked, arms up slightly, as if to fend off a blow.

McGregor clamped his arm tight around Blake's back. They stumbled under each other, down on the snowy sidewalk. Before he knew what hit him, he felt a fist sink into his gut. At that moment, Blake's face was right up close to his, sparkling with melted snow, balled up with fury.

He pushed back, but again he felt a fist dipping into his stomach. Then they rolled. He tossed his clenched hands into space, catching the bulk of a body at times. People gathered around them to watch.

McGregor began choking. He spit yellow bile into the snow. Sobbing, Blake rolled away, against the iron grating of a closed-up supermarket. McGregor let himself go faceup.

The bystanders, mostly students from the university, walked away shaking their heads.

Blake struggled to his feet and went over to help McGregor, reaching down with both hands and leaning back to pull him up. On the ground was the messy record of their fight, an imprint of McGregor's back and wide swoops from their boot toes.

Both still drunk, they walked to McGregor's apartment. At the apartment they drank hot herbal tea that Joanna made—and the fight became a distant action in another world.

Before he fell asleep that night, McGregor thought he would never forget the dull pain of Blake's eyes as the sky dumped into them.

The train squeezed into the curve of the South Ferry station, the end of the line, a tight fit.

"I knew we were going to end up here," Blake said, getting up. "At the end of the island."

Blake led the way up the stairs. Cavernous and smelly, the ferry terminal echoed violently with the din of the only people who traveled on a weekday midafternoon—the poor and destitute. Bag people loaded down with junk. The homeless. Tight-jeaned kids wandering, killing time.

They sat on a wooden bench in the middle of the room, facing the wide sliding doors above which a sign would light up announcing the ferry's arrival.

A flock of pigeons gathered high in the rafters, waiting for the slightest indication of food below. An old lady leaned down to toss bits of popcorn to the smooth floor, and the birds swooped down to fight over the bounty.

"My God," McGregor said, "I feel like I've been thrown back into nineteen-thirty or something."

"The whole room looks like it's coated in something sticky," Blake said. "It's a long road from Wall Street."

"Uum hum." McGregor nodded. A crowd gravitated knowingly to the doors. A shudder had triggered the migration as the boat lazily thudded into the berth at an angle askew to the rotting pylons.

Two workers shoved open the doors, and the crowd of standing people were vaporized by the bright light coming in through the windows outside the doors. Blake and McGregor joined in the mass movement to the boat, following directly behind the last straggler, an old woman, off-balance with a load of crinkly shopping bags. They went down the creaking floorboards, which seemed tacked together, then up the lowered ramp, covered with rubberized slipproof sheets, onto the boat—neither bow nor stern, just the side that happened to jam into the creosote-covered pylons.

The engine rattled and drummed the metal deck.

"Let's stay out here," McGregor said as he sat down on the bench between the entrance doors to the main cabin. All the other passengers were inside.

Blake stood with his coat pulled tight around him, shifting from foot to foot. The air smelled of dead seaweed, exhaust fumes that wafted up from the tailpipes, and rotting wood. The terminal was only half used. The other berth, next door, had been allowed to decay beyond repair, a pile of broken timbers and pigeon nests.

"Half of New York is dead and unused," Blake said as he studied the wound in the building.

McGregor said, "Do you remember the guy who went wild with the ax on the ferry and chopped up a bunch of people? I can't remember, but I think he killed someone. A cop tried to stop him, or shot him—an off-duty cop I'm sure, they're always off-duty when they get into situations like that."

A man came down and put up the chains. The entry ramps were raised and with a slight rumble of the engines the wide boat squeezed and bumped out from between the pylons, into open water, moving swiftly away from lower Manhattan.

The wind intensified as they left the terminal behind and a wide expanse of water, dark and chopping, opened up.

Blake stood looking very much, to McGregor, like he was poised for a movie scene—a lonesome, morose black man at odds with the city shrinking before him. He was the odd man out, job falling away from him—a round of cocktail parties, poetry readings, contract negotiations.

As they passed the Statue of Liberty, as close to open sea as they would get, Blake sat down.

"Do you want to go in?" McGregor gently asked.

"No, let's stay out here in the fresh air," Blake said. "It feels good to be out here and away from that place, doesn't it?"

"It does," McGregor answered. "The boat moves so fast. You're halfway out before you know it."

McGregor put his hands on his knees.

"I don't know what's happened to us, since the fight I mean. And this thing with personnel, I mean you're not connecting with anyone in the office. Well—you know. I don't have to tell you what's been going on with Jacobson; if anything, you should probably fill me in."

Consciously, he met Blake's eyes: "I want to be a good friend to you. And since that night, you've been lost to me."

Blake stood up and walked over to the railing, tilting his head up at the sky. Manhattan looked far away. Gulls still followed the boat wistfully, anticipating food.

"You know I've been trying to sell this Hanson novel, right?" Blake said, raising his voice over the wind. "And you know I think it's damn good. It's the one you always knew you'd get—the classic. And you knew it was going to be a hard sell, because it was a classic. But how hard should it be, actually? I don't know if it's being rejected because it's about a black man or black experience, or because it's just too goddamn good."

"Maybe it's time to let go of it," McGregor said. "That's the painful part of the job."

"Let go. Let go. Maybe you're right. That's exactly what Jacobson said—let go of it Blake. Now. Maybe we should all just let go of these things. Let the rejection letters bow us down: 'We did a black novel recently,' or, 'We found this to be a moving portrait of the black experience'—never a moving novel of human experience—'but it just isn't right for our list.'"

"I still don't know what happened with us, Blake."

Blake turned to look at McGregor.

"I know you don't McGregor."

"If it was that fight we had. Then I apologize, again. If that's what it is, I'll be glad to say I'm sorry. I didn't mean to pry into your life."

"McGregor," he said, pulling his body up a bit, "both of us were drunk. Both of us happened to allow ourselves to punch our true feelings out. But the truth be known, it was more than that, of course."

"Well, tell me."

"I can't. Part of it has to do with you wanting to know things in the first place, wanting to walk in my shoes, my muddy, shucked-up boots. You wanted to know just so you could know."

"There's nothing wrong with wanting to know someone."

"Let me put it this way, maybe my history is the key to friendship with you. Maybe. Maybe not. But who do you want to know? And why? What makes you want to know me, and not some other Joe on the street—now I know what you're going to say. Don't say it. You're gonna say I'm being ridiculous. Maybe I am. Maybe that's why I can't explain it, because it comes out ridiculous, it's based on the ridiculous, on those boots I keep seeing, on where I'm from."

McGregor shifted his feet. "But it's more than that. Isn't it? A lot more. I mean with personnel and everything."

"That's just it. You want it to be more. But my situation," he said flatly, "is no different and has all the difference from yours."

"What do you mean?"

"Face it, McGregor," he said, sadly, "basically, we're all in the same boat."

McGregor said, "Well, at least we're on the same boat."

They laughed.

"No, I mean we all are—very basically—we work, earn money, survive, or we don't. Maybe I'm closer to the don't."

Blake let out a long breath. The boat was closing quickly on Staten Island.

Blake continued, speaking in a low voice. "What's in it for you, McGregor?"

"What's in it for me?"

"Knowing these things, anyway. I mean what's in it for you?"

"I really don't know what you're talking about," McGregor said, a little angry. "It would make me feel good. All right? Just make me feel good."

"I don't mean to put you on the spot or to be facetious, but it's something I've been asking myself, around the office mostly; why someone wants to know the nitty-gritty stuff, when you shop, where you buy gas for the car."

"So there isn't anything we can do about it now," McGregor said in a way that wasn't angry, or judgmental. It was just a statement of fact.

"No," Blake said in the softest voice McGregor had ever heard from a man. It was a light brush of air against the vocal cords. "No, I'm afraid—and really, I do mean afraid—not."

When the walkways were lowered back in Manhattan, McGregor and Blake joined the rush up and into the terminal, then down the stairs to the subway platform where the number 1 train stood waiting with its doors open, ready to make its rush hour run into the heart of Manhattan and back out the other side.

When they reached 42nd Street, Blake said, softly, "Nobody owns nothing."

"Is that a question or an answer?"

"Both."

Then, upon the electronic ding-dong and the closing of the doors, he turned around on his way out of the station and gave McGregor, who was looking out the window, a slow, understanding nod of his head, and lifted his hand to wave good-bye.

The Strange Circumstances of Mr. Woodrow's Death

July 2. Drake liked all of the men he had to shower at Greenwood except Stevens, who seemed to be one of the reasons the word *curmudgeon* had been introduced into the English language. Stevens hated to be touched, actually flinched away from it. The other guys in the nursing home craved kneading fingers, on the neck, or the knee, it didn't matter where.

Under the water Stevens tottered alone, grasping the chrome safety handles along the wall, speaking in a crabby voice, repeating, "You're never too old to die you know, damn it all." Slack-jawed, he let water pour across his face and into his mouth as he spoke, producing a gurgling sound.

Drake did not answer. Stevens's age had played a cruel trick on him, reduced all his knowledge to a few angry facts and swept away the past. Only once had Stevens talked about his past, in a nasty comment: "Why don't you get yourself a good desk job, boy. Like I did." Once that was out, it was up to Drake to fill in the blanks, and he felt compelled to dig a little into Stevens's life.

A quick check in records showed that Stevens was in the army between the two big wars, before he settled down and worked fifty years for State Farm Insurance. "Forced retirement" was underlined in blue on the form. His wife, Rose, died in an auto accident in 1957. His only daughter, Rosette, lived with her husband, Ronnie Alldridge, on an army base in the Philippines. The form mentioned that Stevens enjoyed two hobbies, shooting billiards and assembling model ships. But since Stevens arrived the billiard table in the rec room had remained covered with a tarp. And the only model ships Drake had seen, of the USS *Iowa,* and a PT boat, were gathering dust in Stevens's chickenwire storage cage, in the back, on top of a dingy army locker. (Drake and Artison Chore, alias Artichoke, alias Choke, Greenwood's maintenance manager, tried to use a hammer to crack the lock, but it wouldn't give.)

"Just stand and be at the ready to help. But don't interfere with any 'life-style' patterns," Mr. Matson, the director, told him during the job orientation.

Mr. Matson was comical and small, like a leprechaun; crowned with a ring of red hair, with a bald spot that glistened. Only thirty-five, he looked past fifty, and when they shook hands, Drake noticed big freckles on top of his knuckles, dark, round, the color of plums. Still holding Drake's fingers, he said, "This job is going to be good for you. You'll be able to touch these men's lives in a number of simple but important ways. In a way, you'll be the lifeline to the world of youth; believe me, some of them think they're still your age, and a few of them are, at heart."

Old at heart, slowed with arthritic pain, Stevens moved cautiously from under the water, the slope of his stomach dripping, the hair on his chest as white as phosphorus. His toenails were long and cracked. The hair on his legs was gone, replaced by a network of blue-purple veins.

"You'll be like this too someday," he said, unprovoked.

"Maybe so. You need your toenails clipped."

Drake had the whole thing memorized: boxer shorts worn threadbare, a ribbed tank undershirt, trousers, shirt, socks. Putting on his socks—with the outdated elastic garters that took at least five minutes to put on. The garters burned crisscross welts on his legs like a charbroiled steak.

"Don't hurt me none. Clipping them is what hurt me."

"What about those garters? Those look like they hurt."

"I've been wearing them since I was twelve."

"Same pair?"

It was a struggle to button up his shirt, to get the right angle and enough force against the fabric.

He watched Stevens primp in the mirror, present the perfect, ivory dentures in a strained smile, picking food— breakfast—from the metal clips with his fingers. He said the word "done," and, with a kind of fraudulent joy, turned to the door.

"That was exciting," Drake said, facing the fresh cold air in the hall.

Drake let him fumble, ignoring his own impulse to lend a hand. The sun came through the window at the end of the hall, cast Dawson's legs into long shadows, wobbling, shaking, staggering out of his life.

July 18. Drake listened to Mr. Woodrow the same way he had listened to his mother right before she died, carefully, hopefully, but finding himself unable to respond with words. Woodrow flung himself at his past, loosened the memories from its hard-packed macadam. Unlimited stretches of old roads had filled his life, checking gas pump meters for The Standard Oil Company for a living—Conrad, Lakeview, Kalkaska, Charlevoix—towns big enough to rate a full-service gas station.

"Yeah, yeah. I recall. I did me a station once in Oregon where the old lady who owned the place, and she certainly wasn't no *old* lady by any means—and her husband, thank the Lord, was long dead—took me right by the hand upstairs to a room above her station, all dusty, packed full of wiper blades, maps, and the like; she put me down on the floor, lowered my braces from my shoulders, and bang, we did it right there. If I recall, her name was a Basil Smith. And if I dare say, I remember I found her meters needed to be fine-tuned in more ways than one."

His laugh took firm hold of his torso until he could hardly stand. Drake stepped in, held him by the waist.

While the two men laughed, Choke slipped into the room. Drake felt the air-conditioned air from the hallway coming in with the smell of smoke. When he wasn't striding around in his tool belt, trying to keep things running, or sunning himself on the roof, Choke often came into the shower stoned to catch Dawson's stories.

"Well look at you two," he said while Drake stepped from the shower with his shirt off, the cuffs of his wet jeans rolled. "You got right in there with the old guy."

"Yeah." Drake shrugged.

"Hi Artison." Stark naked, Woodrow let the water drip down his leather skin, making no motion to cover himself or get a towel, staring hard at Choke.

"It's Choke," Choke said.

"To me you'll always be Artison." Woodrow did a little tap dance on the floor mat and shifted around to show his sagging rear end, giving it a sharp little wiggle, like a stripper. Bending down further, he touched his toes, cracked the bones in his back, mooned Choke and let out a long hiss of gas.

"Oh man, I'm out of here," Choke put his hand to his mouth. "Come down and buy some vitamins from me. I'm broke."

"Showing your ass to his kind usually does the trick," Woodrow said when Choke was gone. "Before you came, he had to shower us."

A fast dryer, spinning a towel into a rope, hooking it behind, he made a brisk, back-and-forth motion, scrubbed quick between his legs, armpits, sides, rear end, between legs again, behind knees and neck and feet.

He covered his body with powder, even the tip of his cock, which he waved at Drake like a rope.

"I may just lasso me a lass with this thing."

It looked like a dead snake, like an old candy wrapper. "Yeah?"

"Why the hell not? I'm as ready and able—well at least as ready—as any man you've seen."

This was Dawson's way of poking into Drake's life.

Old hearts work hard. Dressing was the silent part. Breathing was the music in the Greenwood home, open windpipes, lungs wheezing. Drake listened close. It was a song he loved.

Footsteps went overhead. Choke was up in the deck chair getting stoned, taking in smoke from his bong and holding it until his face was red, and blue smoke leaked from his nose.

July 19. Emma Curts died. No longer would she flood the halls by flushing her dresses down her toilet, along with her yellowing girdles, ancient brassieres, and the designer panties her granddaughter brought. Her emerald green eyes had whirled like handblown glass and reminded Drake of his mother's. Emma liked to hike her skirts high enough to show her knees—firm, beautiful, shaved shiny clean—or, if that didn't work, hike them further to reveal the tops of her thighs, the support bands of her beige hose.

The rain began in a blast of thunder and lasted a week. A willow tree near the parking lot lost its grip and tumbled over, crushing Choke's VW Bug. During the rain Drake found himself at Dawson's cage, staring at the junk stored there: two sets of wooden skis with leather strap bindings, a large dresser, an overstuffed La-Z-Boy recliner, a black Schwinn bike with baskets on the sides stuffed with vases, glasses, a pipe rack, old pipes.

July 23. When the river was cresting and Emma was gone, Anna Brisk edged into Drake's life. After Matson shifted her from the night shift to the day shift Drake began to find himself in the same room with her. She had hair cut short, dyed dark purple around the ends. Her cheeks were exotically narrow and pale, below amber eyes, as brown as a beer bottle, and her hips moved around in the shortest, tightest white skirts available from the uniform distributor. Drake knew that every day she brought big bunches of flowers from her father's greenhouse—wildflowers, blue chicory and bindweed, forget-me-nots.

"You have a nice face," she said, kindly, eating a honeydew melon, sitting across from him at the table in the break room, slicing it up into neat sections. In the corner Matson was making tea, shaking the bag, letting the cup catch the last drops. Drake felt a lot was riding on his ability to meet the openness of her gaze, so he stared her down while she rubbed a tiny scar on the side of her nose (he learned, later, a birthmark had been surgically removed).

"Was I too blunt?" she asked.

"If being blunt means saying I have a nice face, I can handle it," he said.

That night the road led to Lake Michigan. One of his headlights was out, and the two lanes were dark; he strained to see the thin yellow line as it cut to the west, into the rolls of dune. The dark shielded his face. He felt lucky. Nobody was on the road. The air smelled of roadside weeds.

She mentioned her father's greenhouse, and a grand-mother from Czechoslovakia who arrived in Michigan alone, having "lost" her husband in New York, and had to pick celery to make ends meet. From that point on she didn't talk all that much, a few comments on a guy named Jackson who had to be removed from the home that after-noon and sent to the hospital when his voice suddenly went—"Like turning down the volume on the stereo," she said, "it just went away while he was talking, faded out." Her own voice faded. The radio played a barrage of old songs from the Seventies with choruses of falsetto voices and disco drum patterns spinning under the melodies.

"Don't go all the way to South Haven," she said when the dunes began to rise invisible around them. A few scrubby pines pushed up against the roadside, closed in on the road. Soon the trees would be gone, replaced only with the bare sand.

"No?"

"No. Let's stop someplace around here. There," she said, pointing to a brush-covered dirt road, leading to what he thought might be an old, shutdown beach house, or maybe just a dead end.

The brush scratched both sides of the car as he eased it to a stop. No sign of a house.

"This is perfect. I can't stand the hang-out crowds along the beach on Friday night."

Looking out into the brush, under the milky starlight, he said, "I remember coming out here to drink beer."

She had on only a white T-shirt, the cheap thin kind that are practically translucent, tucked tight into the waist of her jeans. When she talked, he could see her chest heave, the flat plane of the cotton drawn down from her breast.

"Poor Jackson," she said.

"Poor Woodrow."

"And Stevens."

"Not to mention Chester, or the ladies, Mrs. Cole, Miss Kelly."

"Yeah. Wasn't Mrs. Cole like Stevens. She fought so hard."

"She fought hard, but never like Stevens in a way. He just doesn't give up. Does it ever bother you, Drake?"

She twisted around, tucking her leg up against his, one arm on the steering wheel.

The tip of her tongue surprised him, as her fingers fumbled quickly at his belt. He felt the tiny patter against his ribs, the hardly audible struggle of a cat's heart. The T-shirt was rolled into a necklace. His jeans were stuck below his knees. Eyes closed, he thought of Emma Curts.

He followed the same yellow line back, keeping his one headlight near it, listening to her sing along with the radio in a ragged voice, just off key enough to sound authentically country.

"Daddy Daddy, what have you done to me," she sang.

When the Chicago station faded to static, as they drew near to their inland town, she snapped it off and sang a song she made up as she went along about her daddy, the flowers, a jack-in-the-pulpit wedding. She stopped and said, "Some people say I'm as good as Linda Ronstadt."

"Some people are right. And you always get the flowers in there somehow, for your father's sake I suppose."

"Sure. A jack-in-the-pulpit is a weed, I think."

Entering the outskirts of town, she made up a new song about geraniums and nightshade, about the orchids so rare her father couldn't afford to grow them—about lady's slippers on wooded slopes and common evening primrose along the roadside.

August 16. Choke delivered the news with a pointed smile, an edge to his voice. "That prick Stevens is dead," he said without lifting his head from the air conditioner he was working on.

Drake went to give Woodrow his shower. It seemed like the best thing to do.

As he removed his boxer shorts, Woodrow began a song about a Doggy in the Window, giving operatic flourishes to the last verse, a long, sustained crescendo on the final sustained note.

"Great, great song," he said. "Are you all right?"

"Yeah."

"Stevens's time came," he said while Drake was rubbing his back with a sponge, moving it gently in small circles.

"How do you know his time came?"

"Well, he's dead isn't he? So his time came. Harder," Woodrow said. "You never do my back hard enough."

He began to sing again in a kind of yodel, the water gurgling in and out of his mouth, "How much is the dog-ee in dee windo?"

"You don't like my singing do you son?" he said, drying off. "You don't have to, you know. When you're my age you can go ahead and sing whatever the hell you want— even that punk shit—and the way you want."

Lightly, he snapped the towel at Drake and said, "Are you getting it off of Anna?"

"It's not like corn or something; you don't harvest it."

"Want to bet? I call it good stuff, hot and sweet. You two take to each other nicely." Talc splashed in the air, on his foot, on the floor. His nails were blunt across each toe, nicely cut.

"I've been waiting for you to say something."

"I would've said something sooner, only I just found out about it this morning. Anna helped me eat my breakfast. Sat right there on the edge of my bed and told me everything—sweet little thing."

Drake wanted to tell him something intimate, but the only thing he could think of was his mother's death—and that seemed kind of petty against Dawson's life and the stories it produced. So he kept his mouth shut and listened as Woodrow began again to sing in his shaking vibrato.

August 23. It was an easy death, performed with authority.

As usual, Choke broke the news.

"Another one bites the dust," he said, smiling.

"What do you mean?"

"Your friend Woodrow kicked off this morning watching the *Today* show."

"No."

"Yes. His heart went." Choke's eyes were tiny, glassy, stoned.

Drake passed through the smells of rubbing compounds, soaps and cleansers.

From Choke's office he got the key. Moments later he was deep in Dawson's La-Z-Boy, tilted back, leg rest up, chicken wire shimmering on all sides. From the rafters curls of aluminum insulation drooped at the rotting shoes, mothballed ice skates, the crates, love seats, china, and baseball bats. He said to himself, "Woodrow, you old shit."

When she came up, Drake imagined what Anna was seeing and it made him laugh. "What month is it?" he said.

"Get out of there," she ordered softly. "That's sacrilegious."

Through the wire of the cage, he could barely see her face.

"Yeah, man," Choke said, behind her, hidden in the darkness. "Doing up a dead man's chair just is not right, man."

"What are you Choke, some kind of expert on how to respect the dead?"

Drake stepped out of the cage.

"No man," he said, moving into the cage himself. "I just got to get to work cleaning this shit up, and don't need anyone else messing it up. This is a job, man." Taking hold of one of the skis, raising it up, he broke one of the leather bindings, a splash of brown dust.

"How fucking sentimental. Wood skis. Can you imagine? Damn wood skis."

"Let's go for a drive," Drake said, turning away.

The sun was hot but still low against the trees. Driving was nothing but an excuse to move across earth, to embrace the familiarity of the old road to the beach, past blueberry farms, shabby orchards—attempts to cull a desperate living from sandy soil.

"Driving is an addiction," Drake said. "The speed is a drug to my heart."

Opening it up, he cut his father's old Volvo into the road, felt the sway of oncoming trucks.

"I can't count how many times I've driven this route," he said, keeping his eyes on the road, one arm resting on the sill, his sleeve fluttering.

"Me either," she said.

She watched his arms work the wheel—small, intricate movements flexing his muscles far up his arm. One quick jerk, one wrong movement on the narrow road and it would be all over. She thought about trusting your life to your own two arms.

"This time I feel like I'm driving into something," he said, "not away from it."

His attention locked on the flow of land beside them, burger joints with green picnic tables, blow-up toys, beach towels.

"I'm not going back to that job," he said as the tires hummed over the drawbridge grates and they entered South Haven.

"No," she affirmed, sliding close. "No, I don't think you should go back."

It was a lake town, in the center of the country, but there was a form of seaweed that gave off a smell of the sea. Boats were hauled up onto metal frames so their bellies could be scraped clean.

People worked hard, Drake thought, to draw whatever fish remained from the huge lake. A few hundred miles to the south, Chicago spit out luxury boats by the hundreds. On lazy trips to nowhere people had to stop somewhere like South Haven. The town seemed like a good place to find a cheap hotel and settle down for the night, to end his job with the nursing home. The months had passed quickly. Time didn't wait for anybody. It just kept coming at you like the lines along the road. Anna was singing, splendid lyrics coming out of the blue, howling and hooting, made up from scratch.

Her Story with Mine

We were out in the blue air and it was very late for me, later than I'd ever been up at the lake. We stood there silently, watching our breath pull out from our lips, touch the air, hover momentarily before dissipating.

His big mitted hand was near and I wanted badly to clutch it to mine, to feel it engulf my hand; but I just stood, manly as possible, wondering, worrying, thinking of her out there in the middle of the lake—maybe—or on the other side in the cabin sipping beers.

Treech shifted weight and crackled the snow. He was no longer angry, really, he was standing with his girl's kid brother, searching for her, and he was happy to do so, to make something of just another endless high school Saturday night. From far off, distant, muffled and distorted by the fibrous dry snow, came the whine of snowmobiles.

"Come on," Treech shouted into the air, pulling me by the arm across the ice and onto the lake. We were crossing a rutty span of purple ice, heading north toward the hilly land to a barren patch of sandy brier called Crows Neck, a perfect space for drinking, building driftwood fires, killing time.

He was strong, big and persistent as he led the way before me. His Eskimo parka made him look gigantic with the large hood up, covering his face, sticking way out and making his head rectangular. He was breathing hard as he walked. I struggled behind him. Beneath us, thirty feet of water shifted under a half foot of ice; the lake sighed. We paused, listened, then moved on.

We approached an ice fishing hole, steaming and gushing water, licking the ice.

Treech pulled me wide of the hole, paused to point at it and tell me it was treacherous, likely to crack around the edges at night when new ice was forming.

Five minutes later, we were in the center of the lake and the light was an incredible violet iridescent glow rising, blooming as if from the concentrated light of many stars.

"How're ya doing?" Treech asked me, looking down blankly from his hood, his face dark.

"I'm okay," I mumbled.

"You're a tough kid," he said, pulling me along again. "I'm gonna find your sister, have a nice talk with her. We're going to mediate this problem. Do you know what that means, mediate?"

Before I would answer Treech answered—"It's kind of

somebody who comes between and patches things up, fil-
ters the shit out."

He paused, thoughtfully tilting his head to the side,
then continued, "Hell—that's not it. I just wanted your
company and figured you were good for it."

"Sure."

"Right, you're good company kid. You know things I
don't know, actually. And I'm sure you see things I don't
see. All kids do."

I agreed with him. I could see things here that I'd never
seen before, this being my very first time out at the lake in
the winter, and my first time outside, with an older boy,
hiking, at eleven-thirty in the evening.

He seemed a true friend as he lunged across the ice,
swinging his body forward without fear, absolutely certain of
each foothold, boots crunching, nylon zinging as his sleeves
rubbed his coat.

He was one of me, he was mine for the night; and, like
me, he was being beaten down by my sister's illness. It was
like the lake, deep and murky, very cold, indescribable,
coated over by a thick crust of resilient, ever-shifting ice.

On the lake I thought about my sister. I thought she
suffered from a raw inability to not suffer, to not evoke pain
from every experience of her life, every minute action that
came before her.

She was my sister—and yet—she was not my sister.
Many incidences disqualified her from my love. And yet I
loved her.

Wallpaper: a rich tapestry of small red rosebuds and
thorny vines that Mom picked out for the stairway down to
the living room. I watched the man lay the sheets up,
smoothing the bubbles out with the stiff brush. Damp and
floury, the paste smelled organic and rich as he slapped it
across the sheets, facedown across three sawhorses.

A few days later, as if realizing the beauty and perfection of that wall, my sister kicked holes in it. Fueled by anguish her boots beat through the paper, the plaster, and revealed the ragged slatting behind.

There were no clues, no indications or causalities—just the three of us—Mom, Dad, and me—when we returned from dinner out to see the wall that way. At the bottom of the stairs we huddled and clung. She was gone two weeks.

The wall was patched but never the same. In four places the roses were graceless and unaligned.

"She's sick," my father explained to me; and it was enough, for then, to go on. The destruction of my mother's beautiful new wall, as the destruction of so many other things in our life, had no other explanation. She's sick.

Finally we got to the north shore where a large thicket of sage and nettles reached right up to the edge of the lake.

In summer men came here to fish bluegills from the grouted pockets where the natural springs rise to the surface and the fish sit all day, cooling down.

We shoved our way through the black web of branches, holding them back from each other and softly warning "watch it prickers" when a thorny branch was held back taut like a whip.

Closer now, the snowmobiles turned from a high buzz to a low piston gurgle. Rubber tread ate the snow. Oily exhaust tainted the air and a few shouts, snow-muffled, came up into the hills along with the headlights, cresting into the sky as the machines rollercoasted up and down.

We climbed the first dune hill, our feet sinking through the snow, turning up dark sand.

The machines stopped somewhere in front of us. Treech stopped moving and listened to the silence.

"Damn. I could use another beer," he whispered. "Let's find them."

*   *   *

Pushing off, Treech sprinted the next crest.

"They'll probably have some beers. It's probably Mic and Donny with Kate and Pam. Rentals. Must've rented them down at the Bait Shop in the cove. Think Lou's making some cash that way, renting his Sno-Cats out."

Finally, we looked down into the small valley formed by a mined-out gravel pit.

They were sitting together with the snowmobiles rounded up like a wagon train for protection. In the center, a small fire burned, a few twigs broken from a tree spewing lots of wet wood smoke.

Beers were buried in a kicked-up pile of snow. Everyone sat on cushions facing inward, and from that distance I could see my sister's red down ski jacket. Her arm was up around Donny Steffen's collar, playing with the back of his hair.

Treech went down the hill hard, falling forward while his boots threw up the snow.

When he reached the bottom he shouted in a jovial voice, "Hey man, what's up?" His voice opened up into the thick night, then quickly muffled and deadened in the snow. "What're ya doing," he said slowing down, shifting from foot to foot.

They slowly turned and gazed at us, dull-eyed and silent. I knew Steffen, but the others drew a blank.

"Hi Treech," Donny Steffen said softly. Donny was a big guy, bigger even than Treech, and he liked to fight: At least he was known as a big fighter.

She was looking right at me. Digging my heels to keep my balance, I stayed partway up the hill.

"You twerp," she shouted, "what are you doing out this late. Mom and Dad are going to *kill* you."

"So what."

"I'm going to tell them."

"Go ahead."

"Shut up," Treech said, motioning with his hand for me to come down next to him.

"He came here with me to get you. You were going out with me, or don't you remember that you told me we were coming out here—on the phone, you told me we were coming out here alone."

In the silent air, with everybody around him, the intimacy in Treech's voice seemed unnatural.

"Plus the kid's a buddy of mine, he needs a friend. You aren't his friend."

She pulled her hair from her eyes and threw her head back. In the air her laugh quivered. "You just brought him along to bug me, you bastard."

Out of nowhere, "Fuck you Treech," Donny said, softly. The others sat, staring into the fire. One guy poked it a bit with a twig, blew on it, then leaned back and sipped his beer.

Treech took two steps forward. Snow was beginning to fall again, it clung to the back of his hood, his shoulders, it dusted the black vinyl seats of the Sno-Cats and the golden tops of the beer cans. It was a fine, bitter dry snow that hissed off everything.

Someone sighed, "Ah man, come on," and looked at the others tentatively.

But Steffen, his face ruddy with the cold, glared at Treech. Then he turned his eyes on me and I felt small, tiny and flimsy.

"What's your problem man? Don't you know when the game is up and you lost your chick."

He stood up and leaned toward us.

Casually Treech swaggered over to the beers, tapped a couple with his boot toe, reached down and, with one hand, pulled two of them up, dripping with snow. Then he clicked one open and handed it to me. I took the can from him and drank a cold gulp that burned my throat. It was wheaty and tart, a new taste.

He popped open the second beer and took one long ceremonial swig. His Adam's apple gulleted up and down and then he let out a loud sigh. He looked at Donny Steffen and belched. Then he smiled from behind the hood, a crooked smile that worked its way into his cheeks and formed dimples. Then he belched again, loudly.

"Why don't you get the fuck out of here," she yelled at us. "I hate both of you, especially you. Brothers don't do this kind of thing, they don't."

The cold night was penetrating my jacket, causing me to shiver noticeably; Donny Steffen was restraining himself. He stood, chest punched out beneath his coat, leering at us with hatred. It was such intense hatred that I felt if I hadn't been there, and Treech had been standing alone, Donny would have killed him right off. After all, these were still woods here, deep Michigan backwoods, and Donny had learned to shoot from his father and there was a twelve-gauge strapped to the pack on his machine.

The wind was picking up off the lake, the engines, cooling down, had stopped clicking to themselves and were now silent.

"Look why don't you jerks buzz off now and let us get along with our driving," somebody said.

"But we're still thirsty," Treech yelled to them as he went back to the beers and picked up two more from the pile.

Donny moved now.

"Those are my beers."

"Yeah?"

"Yeah."

"Well these are for me and my buddy." Again he opened the Miller with one hand and gave me my second beer of the night. I was wobbling a bit but feeling acutely brave. Taking on this scene from both a safe distance and from up front where it counted—I thought I would even be able to fight somehow, feel my fingernails digging into Donny's face or knock my sister off her snowmobile and leave her spinning in the snow.

Before I could look up from my beer, Donny had jumped right down in front of Treech and he stood inches from his face.

Treech stood his ground, not moving, subdued by the snow and cold. I saw his legs quiver, buckling a bit at the knees.

"Do you understand," Donny said, "that those are my beers and Katie is my chick now?"

"Those are your beers?"

"You're damn right."

Treech stood up beside him. They were both shaking now, about a foot apart.

"But is this your night Donny? Are these your stars or goddamn lake; or is this your ice?"

He bellowed the words and as he talked he moved back a few steps from Donny.

"You see this is me and the kid's night really, just ours and a few beers and none of you have been here with us. We're here alone. Alone."

Clenched fists at his side, Donny began to form the first punch, pulling his elbow into his side and forming an arched arm.

But before Donny could lunge, Treech grabbed my mitt and turned us both around and we began to walk away from them, up the hill. Donny stood ground, shouting obscenities while somebody started a machine up. The headlight burned our stubby shadows into the hillside.

I glanced behind me down at my sister who was already on her snowmobile and starting to turn away.

We were reaching the top crest of the highest hill. The lake was a large white disk below. The machines whined and were gone, lost in the hard wind that had begun to blow from the north.

Stopped on top of the ridge, looking down, Treech whispered softly. "She's sick, that bitch is really sick."

My throat tightened. I was afraid that I might cry in front of Treech. If I opened my mouth I would cry, if I turned my head and looked into his heavy eyes, I would cry. Doing so would change me in his eyes.

But Treech was already crying, big tears. He rubbed his eyes with his palm and looked down at his boots, shrugged loudly and led the way down the hill.

"It's these beers, you know. They kind of amplify your feelings like that, stop repressing or something like that and then bam, the tears hit."

We were down in the brier brush, and the thickets were shifting in the wind, rubbing the snow. It was falling hard, dulling the edges and biting our eyes. Behind us the machines were lost and so were my sister's friends, whisked away over rubber treads as the headlights carved wedges of light into the night.

Treech's arm latched around my back.

On the ice we walked slower, savoring the night, trying to take it all in.

"And maybe there are still wolves in the woods here, hiding in their caves half asleep with the bears, and even they don't understand the stars."

We approached the center of the lake slowly, the wind, arrived hard from Canada, picked up the powder, swirling it on the ice. It was very late. Treech held me up, his huge arm pulling me along.

"Maybe you'll understand these things when you grow up, take 'em in stride like I do, most of the time."

The dark fishing hole spilled water and sloshed before us; ink black, waxy. We stopped to contemplate its round perfection and the way it stood out with the falling snow; the boot tracks stomped around it almost lost in the dusting wind.

"Panfish still biting down there?" I asked.

"Sure, way down, in the weedy muck on the bottom where it's still warm, a little."

"Yeah."

"That's deep ice kid, the purple stuff . . . takes a two-horse rotor to grind out a hole like that, and maybe an hour."

We swung wide around the hole, retracing our steps. Our original path was almost obliterated by the new snow.

Where the boat landing formed a triangle to the very edge of the ice, we stood on the crust that formed at the edge of the sheet and began to say good-bye to the night in the hard wind; and good-bye to my sister, who seemed lost now, far off in the hills, drinking beer.

On the drive home, I curled up near the heater on the floor of the pickup cab while we swayed down the slippery road. In the vestibule of my house he explained to my father about our trip, saying he was worried about Katie and had wanted to go looking for her but not alone, not at night, not at the lake: so he decided it would be better to have another man along just in case something was the matter.

"Did you find her?" my father asked softly.

"No, not really, but we heard the snowmobiles going and figured they were out hill hopping."

Sympathetically, my father shook his head. His eyes were wide and he looked up at the snow until some hit him in the eye and he glanced away from it blinking.

We stood together while Treech drove away.

I saw him only a few times, later, when I was in high school.

He went to work for a furnace company, folding large sheets of galvanized iron into fitted box-pipe. Once, he came to watch me lineback in the homecoming game on Friday night. In the bleachers, he was hunched over, his elbows propping his head up.

No one found my sister, at least not with my help. And when I was older and visited her in the hospital she seemed calm. She played bumperpool in the lounge; she talked with her friends, her eyes glassy with lithium, dark, deeper, sloshing and dangerous like those ice fishing holes. For now, and possibly forever, I still circle wide around those eyes the way Treech taught me to; and as far as I can tell, so far, neither of us has fallen through.

Anchor
Fishing

On the front step she ate hot corned beef hash from a paper plate. Two speedboats twirled around each other on the lake, trailing russet wakes in the sunset. What induced people to drive in circles out there at the end of the day?

Up close, the boats were graceless gas guzzlers, low-down devices that spit gasoline fumes and oiled the water.

There was a time, she remembered, when she hadn't minded the boats so much, when standing on skis over the wake of water had been exhilarating. One summer she had even allowed herself to fall in love with a simple-minded rich boy from the other side of the lake. He had white teeth and a smooth, tanned complexion. Dapper, in his bright polo shirts, he took her out for glorious high-speed rides in the middle of the night.

She wondered what had happened to him. As far as she knew, he had sunk his beautiful boat into the mucky bottom of the lake.

After her dinner, she settled down to watch a full evening of sitcoms on the old black-and-white set. There were all kinds of happy situations on the shows: cute kids, four or five of them, with a nanny; two cynical but carefree bachelors, no kids; a single father with an adorable black kid, age five. Laugh tracks and jumpy theme songs filled the evening air. Meanwhile, the wailing of the boat engines got lost in the breeze.

After the local news, a late-night talk show came on with a blast of trumpets and trombones. The host was an old man, a comic scarecrow wearing a tight tailored suit. As he talked, his neck jiggled around the collar of his silk shirt. His jokes had a stale aftertaste, and his shirt made her think about her ex-husband.

By the time she had left him in New York, succeeding brilliantly in his career as an architect, he had become as dry and brittle as the starched shirts he brought back to the apartment from the Chinese cleaners, bundled in brown paper, bound tightly in white twine. She wasn't allowed to open the packages.

"No," he said, "I love opening them. It's *so* New York."

Yes, he was *so* New York by the end, patting pink hair goop into his hair in the morning, slicking it tight to his skull, motioning his bright ideas to the sky as they walked up Broadway on summer evenings. His goal was to become as rich, refined, and boring as the other men in the firm, no matter what the cost.

She recalled that day in June when she had moved out, taking the shirts with her. On the way to La Guardia in a cab, she stacked them like a deck of cards on her lap. His number, 98 C, rested in faded marker on the inside of each collar. The tissue crackled beneath the buttons as she flipped through the shirts, each one holding a memory.

After driving through Harlem at 125th Street, her cab got stuck in traffic at the Triboro Bridge toll. A boy in a Mets cap was selling the *Post,* holding a copy of the paper high over his head as he moved between the cars. He came to her window and looked down with dark eyes and a bright smile. His T-shirt was soaked with sweat and clung to his chest.

She began to hand him the shirts one by one. "Take these," she said, "I'm trying to get rid of them and they'd look fantastic on you."

Brooks Brothers, Calvin Klein, Michael Reed, Christopher Hayes, Perry Ellis.

A hint of recognition struck the boy's face and he said, "Man, a Calvin Klein." The wind swept the tissue away as he unwrapped another shirt. "And a Perry Ellis," he added, rolling the name around in his mouth as if he were his best friend. He stacked the rest of the shirts in his canvas bag and shook her hand through the window.

When she turned the set off, the picture curled into a small blue dot which sat there in the middle of the screen, then whizzed off and died. She walked out into the minty air, down to the end of the dock.

It was cool and dark there. She could hear soft music coming over the water—a low, dull bass throbbing under the clatter of crickets.

She walked back to shore, and tried to zero in on the sound. It came from the woods, from the next-door cottage. As she drew near the white birch trees at the edge of the yard, the sound became clearer. A single voice crooned wistfully as a brush swished over a snare drum. The long, strungout bass notes thumped the ground.

She followed the path through the woods, until she stood behind the low-slung branches of an overgrown willow tree. The old cottage was still mostly hidden, but a bug light tossed yellow light over the front yard all the way down to the water.

She knew the place was still owned by the family of auto workers who used to arrive each summer, en masse, in a bunch of old Fords. They worked at the Ford main plant, except for the father who worked at Checker Cab. He drove a huge domestic edition of that car. For three weeks they launched into an uproarious routine. They got drunk all night and roared their rented boat in and out of their dock. In the morning, the father could often be seen hauling a fresh red and brown case of Budweiser out of the boat.

The seemingly inhuman amount of energy this family put into their pleasure frightened her family. They tried to ignore them, but some hot nights, the shouts grew so loud that they pressed their ears against the screens to listen. Between fun and violence there was a fine line—a line no one in her family wanted to cross. So they waited out the three weeks, looking away whenever a boat drifted near their dock.

Now, bathed in the yellow light, a young man sat on the front stoop of the cottage.

She tried to recognize him, but knew that even if she did she wouldn't know his name. She remembered that they wore blue, silver and white Detroit Lions football jerseys with the sleeves ripped out. Even the young ones had had beer bellies over their belts.

He moved slowly in the light. One hand held a beer that he didn't drink. The other dangled a cigarette. He sang softly, his reedy, drunk voice following the words.

Sweet, sweet sorrow, come back to me
I'll give you the lovin'
You'll want from me.

When the song ended, he held the last "me" for a long time, letting it sway up and down off pitch. Then he reached to the cooler at his feet, swished through the ice, and took out a fresh beer. Wiping the water on his shirt off, he twisted it open and drank a long swig. She watched his gullet jump as he drank the whole beer. He didn't have a beer belly, but was lean and trim and strong. She could imagine what a man like this would do with a man like Nash, work him over with his eyes and then, maybe, with his fists. His hands spread out over his knees, flattened like two catcher's mitts, and just as big.

He fiddled with the stereo tape player, turning the tape over and punching the buttons. Accompanied by a guitar, a man howled a simple chorus over and over:

Dreams about you every night
Haunt my awkward sleep
And when I count our many fights
I just break down and weep.

It bothered her—the song. No dreams woke her sleep. That afternoon, she had rowed to the far corner of the lake, working over the horsetail weeds in her brother's old, flatbed aluminum boat, trying to remember something about Nash that would signify the pain she was feeling, lend some solidity to it.

"All lakes," her father told her, "are in the process of dying. The plants grow and die, eating the oxygen, and then, gradually, the lake turns into a bowl of decay. Finally, the lake turns into a marsh, the marsh into a field, the field into woodland."

She said good-bye to the lake that afternoon. She couldn't remember the name of the process that would kill it. It didn't matter, really.

The chorus spun on and on. When the song finally faded, the man stood up, locked his fingers behind his head, and stretched. With his hands still behind his head, he stood for a few minutes, looking out at the water. She watched him while a light breeze ruffled the leaves around her. Crickets sang.

Then he moved quickly, collecting things, taking the tape player into the house and coming back out for the cooler. Finally, he went around plucking up the old beer bottles and some paper wrappers. When the step was cleared, he took one last glance at the lake, and the weedy lawn cluttered with junk—rusted skulls of old engines, a canoe shackled to a tree, an old oil barrel from an unused raft. He shook his head once and went back inside. Seconds later, the yellow light clicked off, and she maneuvered around the black trees back toward the faint light of her own place.

Before she fell asleep, she listened to the boats buzzing on the lake. They'll go on all night, she thought. Maybe it was okay to waste hours of your life, in boats, listening to hokey songs, drinking one beer after another. There are too many wide open hours in a life not to fill them up with meaningless things; and there are too few meaningful things to go around, anyway. This was the last thought of her day.

She awoke under the thin sheet, feeling light, young and rejuvenated. Cool air came through the window. A grainy blue covered everything in the room. She had dreamed of his voice. Delicious and polite, he turned to her from his spot on the front steps and, with his face hidden in yellow shadows, said hello.

This was her last morning alone, she thought. Her brother was returning from a machine parts convention in Detroit. He would bring with him the facts of her life like sticky burrs.

While the coffee percolated in the kitchen, she dressed in a clean, white T-shirt, jeans, and a pair of old sneakers. She went out back to the storage shed where the boat motor was kept, clamped to a board on the wall. Orange life vests hung on long nails. Back in the stink of gas mixed with oil and rotting wood, she found a rack of croquet mallets, several warped badminton rackets, and a clump of bamboo fishing poles rusted together at the joints. Behind all this, she found the blue, fifteen-pound, rubber-coated anchor, still attached to a rolled skein of rope.

She hauled the anchor through the cottage, stopped off at the kitchen to grab her mug of coffee, and then went down to the dock.

Over the glassy silver of the lake, in the blue light, the dock felt a mile long.

She unrolled the line and put one end under her sneaker. With the anchor raised over her head, she spit into the water. Droplets circled over each other. The second time she spit, the fish jumped at the drops, raised their tiny, puckered mouths out of the surface. They were bluegills, pumpkinseed fish.

She threw down hard. The anchor crashed into their mouths. It broke the water open with the sound of breaking glass.

But not a single fish died. They swooped out of the way before the blue weight crashed down. They always did.

So sudden and unexpected was the laugh that came from her that it seemed to shake the weeping willow tree that stood down the shore. It filled her with a sensation of falling down out of herself. With the slimy anchor in hand, she spit again to call the fish back. They came back to the

surface; again she let the anchor fly, even harder this time.
Hauling it up, she threw it again. Their poor snickering lips
continued to come up no matter how many times the tur-
moil replayed itself; they never seemed to learn. With a
snap of twigs, the man next door emerged from between the
branches of the willow.

"Hello," he said, stepping out. He was wearing a cluttered fishing vest. Silver lures flashed from his pockets. In his
hand, he clutched the sections of his fishing rod.

He walked down to the dock. Up close, his face was
clean-shaven and smooth. His bright blue eyes rose out of
his face with their own intensity. He carried with him the
smell of fresh baby powder.

"What'cha doing out here?" he asked, tilting his head
to make the question funny.

She shrugged. To explain a childhood game like anchor
fishing was hard. She wasn't sure herself what the point of it
was, unless you had a grudge against bluegills.

"Gills got to be the stupidest fish around," he said,
looking down at the water. "What were you doing to them,
smashin' them up with your anchor? I thought someone was
drowning over here."

"I guess it's a way of getting out your aggressions," she
said.

"Kind of early to have aggressions," he said, looking
behind him at a band of white light that would bloom into
sunlight soon.

"Actually, it's a game we used to play here," she recalled. "We'd spit for fish and then try to hit them with the
anchor."

He was still looking at the light behind the cottage,
coming up behind the trees. He said, softly, "When I was a
little boy I was sent over here one afternoon to borrow a tray
of ice from you all. It was the only time I ever came over

here in all those years, and I was scared to death of it. Your mother took me around to your back door to give me a couple of trays from your freezer. One froze right to my hand. I cried when she pulled it off, but she was nice. She told me to come on back and play some day, but I never did."

Now she remembered him. He was the little boy with the tiny sharp eyes and the torn-up dirty shirt. Chewing hard on a slab of gum. Snap, snap. "Hi'ya. We get some ice from you all?"

"Why didn't you come over to play?" she asked.

"I don't know," he admitted. "Guess none of us thought we'd fit in talking to the family of a professor. Ah well, that was a long time ago, wasn't it? I was only a kid then."

He was a very attractive man, she thought. There was a kind of beer-ad toughness to his face, but it was very expressive. There were little lines around his blue eyes. His lips never stopped moving.

He hunched down to look in the water.

"Whole bunch right there," he said. "May I?"

She passed him the dripping anchor.

Holding it in one hand, he extended his other hand to her.

"Name's Jake," he said.

He lifted the weight over his head in a quick motion. They counted to three together, and he gave it a hard, downward toss. Spray flew into the air.

Taking turns, one would trick the fish into coming up and the other would make the toss. They worked around the tip of the dock, tracking the tiny mouths and the dorsal fins catching the light. They stirred up the silt until the water was dark gray.

They laughed so much that their bellies ached, and they both sat down to rest.

The sun came up through the trees and hit Jake square in the face. He squinted as he looked up at her so that the wrinkles around his eyes disappeared into his face.

"And you never catch any, do you," he said. His legs were pulled up and his arms out behind him. His ankles, hairless and delicate, seemed out of place on his body, as if his feet had been attached there at the last minute, unfinished.

"Nope, you never do catch them," she agreed. It sounded like a confession. Something slipped out in the tone of her voice—anguish, perhaps. Was she letting it show?

But he cleared things up by saying, "They're stupid enough to come right up to you, but they're smart enough—at least some part of their tiny brain is—to get away."

Jake was on his feet.

"It's been fun playing with you," he said. "I'm sure we'll do it again, soon, but now I have some real fishing to do. It's still early enough so that they'll bite."

They shook hands vigorously.

"This has been lots of fun," he said, holding onto her hand. "I never thought I'd see the day when we'd play together."

"Me either."

Gathering up his poles, he straightened his vest, and marched home along the shore, parting the long branches of the willow like a curtain. She watched until he was gone.

She threw her head back. The lake, free of speedboats, struggled to life in the morning air.

She spit. This would be her last throw. More bluegills came up this time—hungry, horrible fish. Because they were so plentiful, they were called trash fish. Like a pro tennis player making the last serve of the match, she put all she had into it, grunting hard and loud.

She felt the weight leave her hand and fall. The fish curved away from the shadow, all ten of them twisting together like geese changing course in the autumn sky.

Once more, she tried to remember his face. But in the swirl of the water, and the fun of anchor fishing, she lost it, forever.

Jake's Evinrude sputtered to life down the way. She took the anchor back to the shed. The fun, she decided, would have to remain in the simplicity of the toss, and the stupidity of the target.

As Jake's boat cut a swath over the waterfront of her cottage, he lifted his arm up in a long, swooping wave. Then his boat receded to a tiny glint on the far side. That's probably a better way to make a catch, she thought.

Two
Hearts
Times
Two

He remembers the dark clouds, the way the twister pulled down from the sky, poking, hopping, like a natural appendage, making a direct course through town, as if thinking, "I'll just strike her in the heart, run a full course right down the center of Main Street." A tornado is not a funny thing. He remembers that once he had believed all of that mythic fluff about twisters, the Wizard of Oz journeys and lucky stiffs who stared directly up into that winding swirl that was like the very center of hell itself, and lived to tell about it, to brag about it. The real thing brought no such joy. It came out of nowhere, swinging like an iron pipe, and clubbed the town over the head.

But about all Claude Jacobson wanted to remember about that time last spring, and even this was suspect in his mind, was that his son, Johnny, had just about finished with his record-breaking mile race when the storm front began to move in. Digging his spikes into the ash track and ignoring the blood blister festering up under his heel, his son knew damn well the school record was at hand. All he had to do was kick out the last half, and his father would be the happiest man in the state. And he was, until the storm came. The boys scurried to collect the hurdles and cover the high jump pit with a bright blue tarpaulin. Then they hid in the cinder-block refreshment stand—lined with silver tanks of Coke syrup—and waited. The tornado blew apart Gleason's department store where Claude's wife, Bridgette, worked. Sometimes he thought the only true memory he had of that moment was the jockstrap smell of deep heating rub and sweat, the sulfur of foot powder, the wheezing breathing of the track teams.

Claude Jacobson thought all about it, again, for what certainly was the thousandth time. It was Christmas day. He was alone. The smell of cheap cigars, bubble gum, and magazine ink mixed with oily heat in the confines of the News Agency, a place of refuge where each month the external world—dirt biking, sailing, hunting, knitting, politics—slipped into the town from the far reaches.

As he fingered through a copy of *Alaskan Men,* a sort of catalogue for lonely women in need of husky men so strong-willed as to publish their sexual determination, he became conscious of how clunky his name would look there. He thought his name looked stupid whenever he saw it in print, in the church bulletin, or as it had appeared last May when the paper ran a story on the tornado. But the name Claude ran deep into his family. His mother had never allowed him the mercy of a nickname.

The men in *Alaskan Men* weren't any better looking than he was, caught smudgy, printed so poorly their beards—and most had them—melded into solid triangles. The hollows of their eyes were obscured by runny ink, and looked deep and empty, like sink holes. What became clear, as he flipped the pages, was the desperation, pure and simple, in the self-aggrandizing quips:

> Ron Barter, age 34, loves to white water kayak, drive four-wheelers, and build log cabins. Seeks soul mate, woman who isn't afraid to rough it.

Ron Barter was probably the kind of guy who would put an axe through your skull for cutting him off on the highway. Ron Barter wasn't a nice guy, Claude thought, looking at his face, he wasn't a nice guy at all.

Claude slapped *Alaskan Men* back into the rack. Behind the cigar counter, the lady was staring at him blankly. Her problems are the same as mine, the same as anybody else, he thought, eyeing the silver-bell earrings swinging from her lobes. A little sprig of mistletoe was pinned above her breast. For all the good grace of her body, she had a scary, deformed face, as if the powers had pulled a stunt on her, matching a good body with a mask of burn scars that were painful to look at.

The shop seemed to rock with the sway of browsers. In the back, three men were mulling over the "adult" slicks, flicking the pages casually. One man held his magazine tucked inside a *Sports Illustrated* for cover. It slipped, and Claude saw one of those digest-sized things that give a sexual horoscope and contain letters from people who have never done the things they claim, and probably wouldn't anyway if ever offered the chance.

The third man caught and held Claude's eye—Paul

Samuels, a fellow member of the First Baptist Church. Samuels was a widower, too. Discreetly Claude watched as Samuels moved his face deep in a centerfold; like a flasher's, his London Fog billowed around him and he had, Claude thought for a disconcerting moment, the hunched posture of a pervert.

"Help you?" the lady behind the counter asked, her voice loud enough to reach back to the "adults."

"No," he said, quickly, beginning to look over the news magazines in order to look busy. Over the rack, a sign made of shirt cardboard said "No browsers. Buy it, then read it!"

To his right, a kid held a *Richie Rich* comic book, stomped the floor with his snow boots, glanced at Claude, then put the comic back into the rack and selected another one.

Trying to remember what had killed Samuels's wife, Claude continued to gaze over the magazine covers, which all seemed to be concerned with a recent, unresolved hijacking incident. Claude had to remind himself that all of the people—women, men and children—were, at that very moment, still trapped inside the narrow shell of the 747. He could practically smell the heavy, stuffy air, and his calf twitched when he imagined how cramped their legs must be. Three magazines used the same cover photo; a fuzzy zoom close-up of faces in the cockpit window; a gun, blunt and rectangular, pressed into the pilot's face; two of the hijackers looking out at the runway with their faces veiled in black like nuns.

"Anything specific you're looking for?" the lady said again, fingering her sprig of mistletoe and drumming the glass, scratched white from all the nickels and quarters over the years.

The sound of her irritated voice caused a scurry back in

the "adult" section as men replaced magazines and quickly made new selections.

"No," Claude said, turning just enough to get Samuels out of his line of vision.

"Well, you looked as if you were looking for something in particular," the lady said.

"Well, I'm not."

"No need to get snappy. Not on Christmas."

Claude stared at her, holding his eyes on her scarred face until she looked down at the brown cigars under the glass.

Gently, he asked, "Is that mistletoe?" knowing for certain it was because he was a florist.

"Why yes," she said, looking away, this time over the regional newspapers piled on a table near the window.

"Very fresh," he said.

"What?"

"I said it is very fresh mistletoe. Usually it's a bit stiff and discolored by the time it arrives here."

"Oh," she said, "thank you," and she turned to neaten the cigarettes stacked behind the counter.

Feeling vindicated, Claude pulled his muffler tight, buttoned his coat, and walked out into the snow. The street was empty and the light from the store looked brittle against the pavement under the sagging awning.

Any of the stores that hadn't been wiped out by the twister or displaced by competition from the new malls on the outskirts of town were closed for Christmas, Claude thought.

With the snow coming down around him, he plodded north. His galoshes were loose in the heel and made a tiny sound resembling the cry of far off geese. Hanging from the street posts, loops of silver and gold tinsel hissed.

Late nineteenth-century industrial buildings lined the little creek that diligently wove across the town. This was an area Claude had always liked the most. From the train station nearby he had traveled all the way to Grand Central Station and back, an amazing feat it had seemed to him as a boy, an assurance that the town was on the map, drawn into the web of iron rails and right-of-ways.

"Claude. That you?" The voice came out from behind the alley where railroad tracks ran into the wax paper factory.

For a weird second Claude was sure Bridgette's ghost had emerged from the factory.

"That you?" the voice called. "Claude?"

Paul Samuels was a few yards back, standing in his London Fog with a puckered desperation in his face that Claude attributed to the bite of snow on his cheeks.

"Oh, it's you," he said, keeping his voice flat and unresponsive.

Samuels had a brown bag rolled and pressed under his right arm. Claude looked at it and added, "What do you want?"

The London Fog said as much as Claude wanted to know; it was a nice coat but much too light for winter. It wrinkled around his body like crepe paper. Samuels had lost his dry cleaning business in the storm.

"What do you want?" Claude said.

"Not much," Samuels answered. A jitter settled into his voice. "Saw you coming out of the News Agency and I felt I should say hello. I never did get a chance to say how sorry I was about Bridgette."

"That so?" Claude said, beginning to walk again, lightly this time so his galoshes were silent.

"You don't believe me, do you?" Samuels said, pulling himself up parallel with Claude and joining him step for step past the wax paper factory.

Claude looked at the Amtrak sign that had replaced the old New York Central sign years ago. The wood sheets over the windows were dusty gray, but against the wall stood an old baggage trolley with fine metal wheels, a relic from an age of porters, conductors in neat hats and patent leather shoes.

They remained silent as they entered the refuge of the old platform and looked down at the three sets of track rusted a hard ungiving red.

"What you got there?" Claude wondered, looking at the paper bag.

"Just some reading," Samuels said, holding it out. "Here, take a look."

All the good people in the town were safe in their houses as Claude puckered the bag with his fingers and looked down at the shiny paper to see the magazine covers, the exposed flesh, and the bright pink letters that made him aware of what a strange sight the two of them made, sitting alone in the defunct station like a couple of vagrants.

Samuels slumped on the bench and said, defensively, "A man gets lonely."

"On Christmas, especially," Claude agreed.

Together they sat silently until, finally, a squad car made a hurump hurump sound as it went over the tracks to their left, heading to patrol the seediest part of town. The sound set them on edge.

"Better go," Claude said.

"Yep," Samuels answered, pulling himself up. Together they began to walk south, into the wind, along Main.

The snow had eased up. Claude could hear Samuels's teeth clicking like a wind-up toy. His collar had become unbuttoned—or the button had fallen off. All Samuels could do to keep the cold air out, it seemed, was lean forward and keep walking.

Claude unwrapped his muffler and held it out. "Take this," he said, weaving it around Samuels's neck, adjusting it, tucking the tassel under his collar. Samuels stood still while the widower made an attempt to warm him.

There was no place to end up but back to the news shop where the warmth was stifling and the lady behind the counter cast them a hard, suspicious glance. Why were these two men back? While she stared, Claude retrieved his muffler, touching Samuels's cheek with his fingers in the process and tossing the end around his own neck.

"No browsing," she said, "and leave that bag at the counter here."

Samuels placed the bag on the glass and turned to the vast array of magazines.

"Take a look at this," Claude said, holding up the issue of *Alaskan Men*.

They flicked the pages, took in the lonely faces, the blurred ink.

"Sure chop one hell of a lot of wood up there," Claude said.

"No browsing for you two," the lady shouted.

"My ad is coming out next month. It'll say, 'Defunct laundry owner, likes meaningless existence in small town, depressed economy.' Under 'dreams' I'll say: 'Dreams to someday own a new laundry business.'"

A hand came between them, snatched the magazine. "I told you two no more browsing," she said, pushing herself between them, jutting her chest.

"It's Christmas," Claude snapped, "have a heart."

"It is Christmas," she agreed, "and both of you should be home with your families."

"How do you know we have families?" Claude said.

"I see you come in here after church for the *Free Press* Sundays."

"Yeah, so?"

"Well," she said, holding the magazine.

"What the hell." Claude shrugged.

"Yeah, what the hell," added Samuels.

"Get yourself a halfway decent coat," he told Samuels in front of the News Agency, pressing a couple of fifties to his palm. "And take this."

He spun the muffler around Samuels's neck and tucked it back in his collar. "You need it more than I do tonight," he added, pushing a stray clump of fabric under his lapel and then holding him back like a child to see how it looked.

They drove down the same main street and then split apart to reach their respective houses. Claude's was Dutch Colonial, painted stark white; Samuels owned a modern cedar split-level with a hot tub in back.

Both men recalled the funnel that had arrived inland from Lake Michigan and exploded barns all the way, following the two-lane highway—mindfully—and then the flat blueberry farms, rickety fruit stands, and, finally, into the town itself. The department store was peeled open like a can from top to bottom. Shirts, blouses, slips, bras, briefs, socks, scattered across the countryside, hanging from maples, washing down the creek, in schoolyards and baseball diamonds.

President Carter flew over in an army helicopter to survey the damage before calling it a "disaster area." National Guard troops protected the rubble.

Nothing had happened down at the train station that he couldn't account for, Claude told himself. The wiper blades scraped frost and streaked light across the glass. At a stop sign near his house, he pumped the brakes and slid through.

His neck was cool. The muffler looked better on Samuels, anyway, he thought, and he'd give it back in church next week, handing them one more excuse to talk.

For all his trying, he still could not remember what had killed Samuels's wife before the tornado had killed his own on that hot humid day.

Close
Your
Eyes

B y the time Randall got to the
funeral, a simple ceremony at the Congregational church,
the body was being eased out the front door on the shoulders of neighbor folks, people who had known Stan only
slightly, if at all. Nobody *really* knew Stan Needman, but
that didn't keep them away: the church was packed. Even
Mayor Ralph Stangle showed up wearing his best navy blue
suit, nodding with authority and compassion as the men
bearing the weight of a war hero marched past. Since World
War II and Korea, people had to make do with whatever
they could find, even if the deceased was, in most ways, a
complete mystery, and even if the taint of suicide hung in

the air. A medical examiner from Detroit had been called in
to take a good look at the body—a gunshot wound to the
head—but his report was inconclusive, and the cleaning
tools and gun oil lined neatly on the dining room table left
open the implication that the shot was an accident.

The women's auxiliary of the Congregational church or-
ganized the memorial at Stanley's old house out near the
town's fairgrounds, close to the new shopping mall. Randall
skipped seeing the body laid to rest and arrived at the house
early because he'd never seen the place, and he owned it,
or he soon would.

Mayor Stangle was already out on the front porch, leaning his bulk against the rail, having a cigar.

"Tragic," he said through the smoke, "and I've been
told the boy was sure-handed with a rifle."

Randall was not ready to tease apart the facts of
Stanley's death. "Could you show me the letter once more?"
he said? shaking the mayor's plump hand.

"The copy I sent you?" Stangle drew on his cigar, blew
the smoke to the side, down into the azalea bush.

"I left it back East," Randall mumbled.

The mayor reached into his jacket and handed the original over.

Holding it close, he examined the stiff block letters,
written in fading pencil lead, dated two years back:

I HEREBY WILL AND LEAVE ALL OF MY ASSETS AND
BELONGINGS TO ONE RANDALL SCOOT, WHO KNEW
ME HONESTLY. WHEN I DEPART THIS LAND, IT WILL
BE WITH ONLY ONE WAR UNDER MY BELT. MY
SORROW GOES TO THOSE WHO HAVE FOUGHT
SO MANY, DAY IN, DAY OUT.
YOURS,
STANLEY JACKSON NEELMAN

"It's all yours," Stangle said, raising his arms up to the chipped ceiling, "as soon as the court checks this thing over. But as far as we know Stanley had no kin, or close relations, or even friends, hardly. And of course you know his mother's dead."

"Yes, I . . ." Randall began, feeling his heart pound.

"Yes?" Stangle gently interrupted.

"You know I can't seem to recall yet exactly what my relationship was with Stan," he began, "except that he was our neighbor for a time when his mother rented the house next door to ours in town. I was just a kid, though, and I don't remember much."

Stangle clapped his heels down on the wood floor and glanced around at the cars arriving single file, with their lights on. "Yes I remember that house. I managed the taxes and mortgage on that one for the owners. They wanted the Needmans out. Thought the old lady was a bit strange. She might burn the place down accidentally or something. And the burden of talking them into allowing Stan and his mother to stay rested squarely on my shoulders, believe me. But I always believed those people should be treated properly, that is until Stanley left his mother alone and moved out here to live. Little did I know that he'd been saving up his VA payments so carefully."

With that he stood up and went to the stairs to greet his "constituents," who seemed to skip eagerly from their cars, lifting dress hems, adjusting ties and collars, brushing stray hairs into place.

During the beginning minutes of the party Randall did his best to brush questions away by staying with the men in the heat of the front porch as the ladies whirled dutifully about with trays of Ritz crackers and cans of Cheez Whiz.

Past two large azalea bushes, beyond a scrubby bit of useless field, loomed the back of the Westridge shopping mall. It was Sunday, and the mall was busy. Even the back parking spaces were filled. From the house, the rear of the structure—unspruced someone called it, lacking the fake marble tiles that adorned the front—looked strangely like a sinking battleship, falling into a sea of weeds and heat.

"I'll never understand how a man could do that," Al Lerner, who owned a bootery downtown said, chewing a cracker, "either shoot himself accidentally or do it intentionally. Either way appears equally foolish to me."

"Happens all the time," Ned Allison said. Ned owned the Citco station at the bottom of Westgate hill. Allison had lost a leg in the Battle of the Bulge. In its place, a prosthetic device made of plastic too pink to look like skin was strapped onto his thigh with a series of leather braces. Once, Randall remembered, back when he was a kid, Allison had shown the whole thing to him. Better artificial legs had long ago been invented, he explained, but he was sticking with what they gave him after the war; to tack something new on like that you might as well be taking off your *real* leg. A man gets used to about everything, he said, and attached to about anything too.

Ned was staring at Randall as if reading his mind, locking his head at an angle, out toward the sidewalk, a gesture indicating his desire to go for a walk.

"Walk?" he said.

"Yeah," Randall concurred.

Esther, Stangle's wife, had opened the screen door for the men to move into the living room. She had been hovering close to her husband with a tray of wheat crackers, talking in a hushed tone, wearing her slim black dress with frail lace around the sleeves and collar, as chic as one might find in the town. The men gazed openly.

She was at least fifteen years younger than Stangle, Randall knew, and worked in the "intimate apparel" department at a branch of a Chicago department store in the new mall. Most agreed she had married Stangle for his money. It was good to step off, to walk at the leisurely pace forced by Ned's plastic leg, thrown forward at half speed. The sun pressed down, and the dry hiss of insects came from the overgrowth.

"So," Ned grunted, out of earshot of the house, "you're making it big in the city I understand."

"Yes, sir," Randall said, figuring his father, who was up north fishing, updated Ned on his life whenever he went in for a fill-up.

"Good, good. It is a fine thing to strike out on your own like that."

Randall thought something was wrong with the comment, coming from the side of the old geezer's mouth, fuzzed with a strip of whiskers he had missed shaving. It sounded as dull and flat as the landscape around him: The old maxim was worn threadbare by use, by the reality that there was no longer any place *desolate* enough to really "strike out" *into.*

"Nam," Ned said, pushing it like a cuss word, the sound of an iron skillet landing against the soft side of someone's head. "You were about sixteen at the time he came back."

"That's about right. I just got my driver's license."

The answer gave Ned pause. He stopped and adjusted his leg, reaching through the holes he had cut in the bottom of his pockets to get at the straps.

There are only a few ways to remember anybody, Randall thought, and memories get strapped onto you like Ned's leg, with all kinds of leather belts and cold chrome buckles leading to one simple thing.

Before he went to war, Stan Needman taught Randall how to throw a spiral pass like Johnny Unitas, if not better, by lining the ball's white stitching up in his palm and letting it slide out over the curled fingers, holding your arm and hand the way a waiter holds a platter of food, sensing where the ball should go, almost willing it there.

He had even said "will it there." Smelling of Brut 33 aftershave, he was trying to impress some girl waiting for him on the porch that afternoon, to show her that he was the gentle sort of guy who was willing to put his arms around a kid and teach him football.

"Will it there."

The sidewalks on that side of town were cracked, pushed open by the swelling roots of ancient long-gone trees. The company that laid the cement had pressed its name into each section: Bronson Cements, Bronson, Michigan, 1920.

Now poor people lived in the weatherbeaten Victorians, and not a single home had complete windows, or a porch railing without a missing slat. The only thing that kept that side of town from falling to complete ruin, Randall thought, was the mall, which acted as a kind of economic dam—at least that's what the town fathers, who had approved the project, liked to say—by employing people at menial wages, manning the cash registers and working the budget warehouse stock rooms.

"I wish I might get a quarter for every story I'm going to eventually hear about what really happened to Stan Needman," Ned was saying, "and about why he left *you* his estate. But I suppose this might fall into the category of things without an explanation."

As if to put the emphasis on the absurdity of his own plight, Ned gave his fake leg a hard slap. "But what the hell. A good mystery sparks the town up anyway," he added.

A good mystery does more than spark a town, Randall knew. People demand answers. His return to the party

would put him face to face again with Mayor Stangle, Al
Lerner, Esther, and all the ladies, teacups poised. They
would want, sooner or later, to hear some words of memorial to Stanley, a story to validate the ceremony and efforts of
the afternoon. Because in the absence of some concrete reason behind Stanley's gratitude toward Randall, a story would
have to be created to fill the space; and Randall was pretty
sure that *any* story the town made up would be far from the
truth. Not that these folks were of a bad sort, he thought.
They just grew tired of the day-to-day pleasantries and had
to focus once in a while, when possible, on some rumor or
strange action to which they could nail their hidden anguish.

"I've seen men come back and burn their own houses
down." Ned was speaking, gently scratching his thigh as he
walked. "Stranger things have happened to be sure."

There had been minor attempts at festivities when Stan
("our boy") returned from Vietnam. A few rolls of white ribbon were strung from the oak in the Needmans' yard to the
elm in the Scoots'; a makeshift sign was crayoned by some
kid; the pastor from the Congregational church, Jacob Killington, showed up, along with some of the same folks who
would, years later, attend the memorial.

His return was like one of those scenes in the movies,
Randall remembered, when the sun brushes tears down
cheeks and the whole thing swoops along in a kind of stupefied slow motion. Stan's face was acceptably battered and
stubbled in the way one expected of a war hero. His medals
swung from his T-shirt. A sleek little scar cut up from his
chin into the high part of his cheek, and the first thing he did
when he got out of the station wagon was lean down to
stretch out his gimp knee. The ligaments had been torn apart
when he fell, playing touch football at some jungle base.
With a dramatic thump, he dropped his duffel at Randall's

feet and went over to kiss his mother, holding her gently, on the porch, just outside their front door.

Norma Needman was usually housebound, secluded inside, blinds drawn, television running all day, for, most said, no damn good reason. Mrs. Scoot agreed and refused any part in talking with Norma.

The death of Stan's father in an industrial accident at the Stonewood paper mill was ancient history, Randall's mother explained. The great "widow maker," they called it, because "so many were lost." But it wasn't excuse enough to ignore the good people of this neighborhood and sit inside smoking those fancy cigarettes, the ones made for ladies, long, slim, coming in elegant green packs.

Now some black kids were playing in a yard near the corner of Stanley's street, chasing each other around. Ned turned to Randall, grunting with the force of his stilted walk.

"Didn't Stanley have a black friend right after he came back?"

"Maybe," Randall said, looking at the house on the corner, falling into itself, eaten by weeds. Time messes things up, it surely does, he thought. The kids disappeared into the thick bushes along the side.

"Yeah, that Negro boy," Ned was saying.

"Yes," Randall answered, "I remember that guy now." And he did.

The guy's name was Kofi Phillips, but he decided it was not time to give it away to Ned.

"A big troublemaker, he was," Ned insisted with a sniff, eyeing the back end of the mall, rising up like a submarine as they moved down the street.

Kofi was thin as a reed, and with a kind of dainty walk, cautious, like a dancer, pushing off with his toes. He had appeared on the porch one day, drinking iced tea with Stan.

He remembered trying to pretend to be busy, walking

quickly to his front door only to be called over for an introduction. Kofi was an old buddy from Nam, Stanley explained, come over from Detroit to visit for a while.

"That's right," Kofi confirmed, nodding at Randall, his words so soft. Never had he seen such a mouth. Kofi's lips were purple and as shiny as grape leaves, and his hair was cut close to the scalp, not like the Afros the black guys on the team wore. And his first name. It was a name he had given himself in the army, just for the hell of it, because he liked the way it sounded, African, traditional.

The two men sat tilted back, chairs on two legs, their own legs up on the railing.

Randall could not remember what excuse he had used to leave them alone, but he knew it had been a bad one.

One afternoon a few weeks after Kofi first appeared on the porch, around the Fourth of July, Randall was sure, because the smell of sulfur was still in the air and out in the backyard there were gray rusted bits of metal, the remains of burned sparklers, Randall drove home on a whim to get a Dylan album Jake Wilson, his best friend and coworker at Pizza King, wanted to play at a party that night. Now, looking back on it, he saw that fate had been at work. The crossing of paths, he thought, listening to Ned drag his fake leg, always entails risk; accidents happen at crossroads. He decided to park the car in the garage that afternoon, something he rarely did, and went to the house through the backyard, passing along the hedge, ragged and overgrown, dying a summer brown in spots, dividing their patio from the Needmans' yard. The dead sections allowed a clear view through.

Kofi Phillips had his lips against Stanley's, just brushing them slightly, and his hands were hooked over his friend's wide leather belt. Framed by the dead part of the hedge, the men kissed not wildly, or even with passion, but with kindness. Stanley Needman had his fingers spread out over the back of Kofi's head as if he were palming a ball. Before he could turn away, the kiss had changed from something experimental to something solid, pulling out like taffy.

Then they became aware of Randall and jumped apart.

"What the fuck," Stanley said.

"Shee—eet," Kofi sighed.

"Sorry," Randall said, remembering the way Stanley had held his arm up into the air like a statue when he taught him to let the ball roll from his palm.

That one "sorry" must have satisfied both men, because they broke out laughing and rolled onto the grass together, Stanley shouting "What the fuck. It's all over."

A few weeks later, near the end of August, Stanley moved to the north edge of town, the black side, and hunkered down with his VA benefits.

Even in high school, Randall knew it was in most men to do that kind of thing under the right condition. So he simply kept his unbewildering knowledge to himself. Maybe he hadn't made enough of what he'd seen, he sometimes wondered. But maybe that was it. Maybe that was all he did to earn the lifetime possessions of Stanley Needman.

Mayor Stangle waved as they approached the house. Randall saw that in the afternoon sunlight the house's disrepair showed acutely. The front eave drooped down and a network of vines climbed the clapboard on the shady side, pulling off what little paint remained, causing some obvious wood rot in spots. Under the cornice, in a support beam, a bird had built a nest, a gray clot stuffed into the wood.

More people—mostly men—lined the front porch, including Reverend Killington, who presided over the service and dreamed up the idea to have a party at the house.

"Well, well," he said, "here's our true war hero."

Ned slapped his pants. "I ain't no war hero Reverend. I run a gas station for a living."

"Now, now," the mayor said, blasting alcohol fumes into Randall's face, "here we also have the beneficiary of this tragic—incident."

A few of the women hovered in the shade of the doorway, behind the screen, and Randall ignored the comment and headed past the mayor's belly, opened the door, and stepped into the front room. Before the door slammed, most of the men had followed him through.

The momentum of the celebration had slowed. Most of the windows were stuck shut from the humidity, so a fan had been set up in one corner of the room and was swaying uselessly. Near it, the huge Zenith television in the corner was on, tuned in to the weather channel.

"Get the boy a seat," the mayor ordered, sounding more like a southerner than a man born and raised in the Midwest.

The church secretary Mrs. Wiggins, her hair packed up in some kind of net, scurried to the front porch and came back with a folding chair, which she placed nearly in the center of the stuffy room. She nodded at it, waiting for Randall to sit down.

As he sat, he searched the room for familiar faces, somebody to save him, and found only Al Lerner, Esther, Ned, and the mayor. This is all too strange, he thought. Except for Esther, whose sleek dress pressed damp against her narrow figure, most were elderly churchgoers the Reverend Killington had rounded up, or a few city council members who knew a good patriotic opportunity when they saw one.

With her face freshly powdered, and the strong smell of expensive perfume drifting off her neckline, Esther came back to Randall with a tall glass of iced tea. It was a signal of sorts, and everyone settled down in one place or another, lining the couch, turning folding chairs in his direction, hunching down into the bean bag chairs.

"Now," the mayor set in, looking at Esther as he spoke, "most of you know Randall Scoot, or you remember that he was the boy who sent our high school team to the state championships ten years ago as quarterback."

He paused as a few heads shook.

"And I'm sure that most of you read in our paper that Randall has been named to inherit the estate of Stan Needman."

On the television screen a radar shot of the United States showed a sickle of clouds driving across the Great Plains toward Michigan, bringing what Randall hoped to be a wicked storm, breaking open suddenly with booming thunder, ending the necessity to explain things to the people circled around him. But the storm didn't come. It was still stuck someplace over Iowa.

Randall took a long drink of his tea and began, lowering his voice to make them listen hard and to fill the void the past left in the room. I've got to fill it up, he thought, anxious to get it over with and get back to New York and the simplicity of the city.

"Well, some of you might know," he said, "that Stanley Needman taught me how to throw a football."

"Boy did he," someone said.

"Yes, he did," Randall said, lifting his hand up into the throwing position. "Stanley taught me that poise and honesty are important in throwing a ball, that you have to let go of the thing correctly—honestly, he used to say, I think those were his exact words. You have to let go of things honestly."

The mayor leaned back to listen, gazing over his gin and tonic.

"By the time Stanley came back from Vietnam, I was

just about graduated from school. For whatever reason, he did two tours of duty over there, and I guess most of us were looking for some kind of change in Stanley when he returned, some indication of what the war had cost him, personally. So many were coming back, you know, scarred—mentally, I mean. I looked along with everyone else to see how the war changed him. But Stanley came back as healthy and wholesome as any man around, if not more so. Or at least that was the way I remember it when he first came back."

"But then he up and moved out to the north side of town," one old man said, leaning against his chrome walker handles, near the fan. Big age spots the color of raspberries spread over his bald head.

Randall felt eyes digging. The television flicked ads—farm products, a wide mower to chop weeds, a club for hair replacement.

"In the Negro side of town," the same man said, arms shaking, "where he didn't belong." He said Negro like two words: knee, grow.

"Now, now," Stangle interceded, using his voice trained to gain control of public forums. "This is no place for that kind of talk, John."

"What kind of talk, Mayor? My son paid with his life in the Big One."

No one turned to listen, figuring it was better to let the voice continue.

"May I," Randall said, firming up his voice.

"Please," someone said.

"Now you all are probably wondering why I'm the one who ended up with this house in my hands. The fact is I'm the only one who knows the truth about Stanley Needman, a truth that he held away from all of you. The last thing he wanted to be was a war hero. But he was a hero. And I'll let you know why. I mean it's a strange thing when the past comes back at you like this. I'm sure you all understand," he said.

"Now, when I say Stanley came back from the war unchanged, I'm just trying to put the whole matter into a kind of perspective. He didn't have Agent Orange, or shell shock, or any of that stuff we know about now. But when he came back he told me stories he swore me to secrecy on."

That got them. Secrecy was understood in Bronson. The knowledge that he might break that oath made his story sound even more truthful.

"One day I took off work early and decided to drop by our house. As I was walking down our back sidewalk, I heard some crying coming from his yard—hard cries, the kind a man makes. This is personal, so you'll forgive my telling you about it, but I want you to know this." His throat parched dry, he lifted his glass for more tea.

"So I hear this crying and I look through the hedge to see him down on his knees, chin skyward, in tears."

Esther handed him a fresh tea.

"I was just a high school kid you know, but I knew that something was happening, and I had some real love for Stanley. So I went into his yard and asked him if he was okay.

"'I went against the beast,' he said, and then he began to tell me the story, the one he made me swear never to tell anyone so long as he was alive, and even after that.

"The whole thing took place in some godforsaken village in Nam, you know, some damp jungle hamlet near the edge of the DMZ—that's what he said. His unit was on a special patrol, sweeping a grid for something or other, and Stanley was point man on the formation, taking the lead, using the point of his rifle to push back the dense brush, keeping his eyes sharp, listening—he said—to the sound his heart kept making on the inside of his ribs, like a small knife cutting in there. Fire broke out. Dense fire from all sides. Tracers. The kind of fire that says ambush, coming down from positions in the trees.

"Now most of the fire was coming from behind him. The ambush had probably waited until he was past in order to get a good clean shot at the rest of the company as they passed. So Stanley ran forward and hid himself in the trees to set up a position from which he could shoot.

"As he got down on his knees behind a tree he felt a long snap in his knee. It just gave out under him, the cartilage torn apart where the bullet entered—you remember the scar. Now here's what he told me, and his friend Kofi confirmed. With his leg hanging by a thread, he made his way through the gunfire to find his unit. Kofi was down. One of the bones in his spine, a disc, was shattered. Pumped with adrenaline, Stanley lifted his friend onto his back and carried him—not a few yards, not a quarter mile, but six miles down the pike, an act which earned him a Purple Heart.

"When he told me this story, he reached up and put his arms on my shoulders. It was a hot day, like today. He said, 'Being a hero is the hardest thing there is. I threw that medal into the Kalamazoo River one night. It's out in the lake by now.'

"He kissed me on my forehead and said thank you, sniffing, wiping his tears. And that was it. That, I think, was the one time I helped Stanley Needman over his suffering."

Strong sobs broke out—first with Mrs. Wiggins, then one of the men Randall didn't know, passing on to a few of the ladies, who had hankies ready for the event, and, finally, with impressive magnitude, Mayor Stangle himself, catalyzed by strong drink. Even the man holding his walker seemed moved by the story. The whole room began crying. A hero was born. The man was a hero. All along we knew it.

Randall got up and left the crying to stand alone on the front porch. For a moment he watched the view of the back of the mall leaning on the wasted edge of the town, cars pulling in and out, a man lifting cans into a big green dumpster, the lid raised like a mouth. Beyond the sky was pasted with hazy heat, waiting to crack open with the coming rain.

"It'll take some work to get the place in shape," Randall thought, glancing at the blisters of paint falling down off the ceiling, recalling, again, the two men rolling on the grass. Kofi Phillips's voice: "What the fuck. It's all over."

The Question of Toby

For the past three months, Thompson had spent his Sunday afternoons with Gladys Janson. Gladys's husband, Russ, worked double time at the Rubbermaid plant on Sundays, so her house was clear. All he had to do was assure Margaret that he was finishing up his parish duties. After preaching the second service, and attending the agape brunch with the members, no one at the church expected him to hang around in the afternoon. Most thought he was home tending to his family duties. The affair, his first, fell together with an ease that surprised Thompson. In only a few weeks he had learned that a small town, despite misconceptions most people had, was really a bastion of privacy.

And shrouded in that privacy the affair seemed mainly one of convenience. Gladys was hardly attractive, a hefty woman verging on obese who wore oversize, draping housedresses, and drank piña coladas to "get herself in the mood." Their lovemaking was controlled by the vast contours and weight of her body. But he liked that. She crushed him with her warm bulk, so unlike his wife's slim, well-maintained efficiency. In another time Gladys might have been a mother to a brood of hard field-workers. But she didn't have kids.

With the affair, Thompson had acquired a tough new resolve. He liked the thought that her husband Russ was a tough guy who would likely put a shotgun to the head of any man he caught with his wife. His guns—and he had many of them—were racked, stacked up in a wooden cabinet in the dining room. When Thompson saw them he felt close to some future point of action at the very fine edge of human reason. The danger Russ posed was no small factor in the equation of their lust, an equation which spit out the right answers with precision each Sunday afternoon.

But then his wife, who had skipped the morning service as usual, called him at church to inform him of his son's strange behavior.

Now this, he thought bitterly, called home to deal with *this*.

"How do you account for yourself, son?" he said, not looking at his boy, Toby, but rather holding his eyes, slightly unfocused, on the blooming honeysuckle bush being picked over by heavy, dark bees out the window.

"I don't, sir."

"You don't account for the fact your mother found you in such an unbearable position this morning?"

Flushed with embarrassment, the boy allowed himself to say "no" again, knowing the possible consequences but still feeling protected somewhat by the fact that he was only eleven years old. He knew his father's piousness was as solid as the wooden yo-yo in his back pocket.

"Did I hear you say no?" Thompson asked reluctantly, not sure yet if he was going to play the role hard or gentle. Child psychology books tended toward the latter. But in this real-life situation he felt it was probably best if he just followed his crude instincts. Trying to remember what his own father might have said, he paused for a moment to adjust the lampshade on the side table.

With his legs hunched under like a crab, his son remained silent.

My father spoke to me maybe three times in my entire childhood, Thompson thought, or perhaps it just seemed that way. Of course those were harder times. For a brief second, the low-down plain house of his father's birthplace came to his mind, cocked hand pump to the side, the relentless Illinois sky pressing down—a dust bowl documentary photo—and then the stern, hopeless face of his father, with the wide mustache pulling his upper lip down beneath thick brows. What would he have said if he found me doing it? Most likely he'd have dug into some boring medical explanation using the jargon of his profession. But the penis itself, and what one could do with it, would have been locked away in some dark vault of his vocabulary; as a matter of fact, as far as he could remember, the word had never passed his father's lips.

Looking back down at his son, he was shocked to see that the boy had his finger up near his mouth, as if pretending he had a mustache himself.

"Get your hands away from your mouth, damn it." Yes, with his finger up there like that he could see, in the shadow, a mustache just like his father's. It brought out the true form of the boy's high thick brows, now as blond as wheat, but already darkening, and the eyes deep in the sockets.

"Say something," he yelled at his son. "Account for yourself."

Sunlight came directly through the purple stems into the room. Did his small lips move? Did he not have some childish way to explain it? Even a foolish lie would resolve something: I was just trying to rub something off, some lint, from my pajamas. It felt good, so I did it. Daddy, I wasn't doing anything.

When Thompson stood before his church, he had no lack of words. Ideas and phrases slid from his tongue as if down a sluice, while the faces in the congregation, all familiar to him, tended to combine as quick as the colors mixing on a spinning top. In seminary, down South, Oratory 101, he had learned all kinds of preaching methods. In a ladder sermon you walk the listeners up the steps of your sermon, leading them up the rungs—of confession—to redemption. In the circle sermon you take them around from sin to salvation, sin and then salvation again, rolling to a stop. The hammer sermon works just like it sounds—begin right off pounding your point, pounding, pounding, until it's hammered home. Thompson swore by the hammer method.

A breeze, sweet with honeysuckle, came through the windows. Trees ached with green buds.

Thompson became aware of how easy it was for him to be embarrassed about the shortcomings of his own son.

"Okay, I'm going to count to three and I want you to give me some kind of explanation for what your momma had to catch you doing up there in your bedroom, son."

"One."

The child untucked his legs and let them flop over the edge of the davenport.

"Two."

He turned his head away, twisting it like an owl, and looked out beyond the honeysuckle. As if to form a word, his lips parted.

"Three."

His tiny sneeze tossed spittle onto the top edge of the window.

Swiping the silver gobs from under his lip, the boy turned his head back around and pouted at his father, quickly, before his mouth straightened firmly.

"Now listen, son. You're hardly a man now. But comes a time when you're asked to account for what you do, to find the words to explain what you do. And this is the time. Do you understand?"

"You want me to find words?" The boy's voice was like a single, high piano note.

"No. Not *find* words. Just tell me what you were doing when your momma caught you up there this morning and, once said, we'll feel better, won't we?"

Fumbling about the couch, the boy made like he was ready to do some more talking, adjusting his small arms under his striped shirt, drawing up his legs again and giving his father a direct look.

Tapping the lampshade again, Thompson waited and wondered if it was true when folks in the parish said Toby was cut from the same cloth as himself. One would think the boy had a couple of his preaching genes, he thought, and would at least be able to put a few words together into some kind of excuse.

"Toby, I'm willing to stand here all day if that's what it takes. Now just spit it out, damn it. This isn't such a big deal."

While he waited, there was a faint tapping at the back screen door, and Burt Harvard, their next door neighbor shouted, "Yoo hoo. Anybody home?"

"Come on in Burt," Thompson called loudly, "I'm in the sun parlor with Toby."

Harvard, a big unwieldy man prone to wearing greasy overalls, ran a bait shop by a nearby chain of lakes. Along the bank of a connecting channel, he made out well with business from both lakes. But as a price, he carried with him a faint odor of worm manure and grasshopper feed that disgusted Thompson's wife. "When you call someone *lowlife,*" she once said, "the Burt Harvards of the world are your prototype." The worms grew in tall humus piles wrapped in snow fencing flush against the Thompsons' yard, another sore spot with Margaret. From a small shed in the center of his yard one could hear a roar of crickets emanating, a high-frequency electric pitch. Harvard liked to say, proudly, "I make my living from life."

"Hi'ya big guy," he said to Toby, winking as he stepped into the sun parlor. Toby turned away to face the honeysuckle, the purple lace shadows weaving his cheeks.

Shifting beneath his overalls, Burt sensed the sober feeling in the room and got to his point. "Need a socket wrench," he said, noticing that Thompson was staring at the couch. "I think I lost mine. Can't get the damn distributor cap off the Chevy. Want to check the points. Timing is off a bit. And while I'm here," he added hastily, "I'd like to borrow that new router bit you bought from Sears. I'm thinking about finishing that hutch for Dawn. She has to have a place for her new china."

Although Thompson felt some gratitude for Burt's intrusion, like a forgiving bell in the first round of a fight, he began to see something in Harvard's sidelong glances—directed to the davenport—that told him the man would be as quick to side with Toby as he was to defend the quality of his night crawlers, or his crickets, or slugs. And Margaret's harsh words kept coming back to him. After all, Harvard called himself an expert on the lower life forms—and even worms, who weren't male or female, mated, he had once explained, by rubbing side-by-side against each other.

They went down to the basement together.

"Let's see, my socket wrench should be around here somewhere," Thompson said, sliding over the powdery sawdust on the basement floor. His workbench was located directly beneath the dark rafters of the sun parlor.

Burt stood under the neon work light, next to the large, gray belt saw, against the carved-up workbench Thompson had U-hauled back from his father's old place in Galvison. He knew better than to begin poking around a man's work space, even with his eyes.

The basement was closed and silent. From the single, low window came a grimy light filtered through the undersides of winter-dead rhubarb leaves that grew untended in that spot each year. Past the leaves, one could see the mat of grass blades, half an inch high, cut last week, weaving into each other to form Thompson's prized lawn.

Thompson quietly searched for the wrench. From overhead, through the house's old floor, against the web of nails, carpenter pencil markings, wires and pipes he could hear the squeak, as faint as a dog wheezing after a hard run, of the davenport spring where Toby sat. A sound twisting like the worms beneath Harvard's humus mounds.

"Okay, let's see. I'm pretty sure it was somewhere just about up here," he said, swaying his index finger like a divining rod, hoping to locate the chrome wrench amid the clutter of tools on the pegboard, his tools, his grandfather's tools, and even a few from before that—handmade wooden clamps. A tart taste came to his mouth. Why couldn't they make things like that anymore? And the socket wrench. It should be hung next to his father's awl.

Upstairs the spring in the davenport was squeaking loudly.

"Look," Burt hesitated, "why don't you bring it over to the garage when you find it. I'll be under the car. Figured I'd change the oil now too."

Hearing Burt's affable voice—nervous, anxious, he noticed that the sigh of the spring was becoming somewhat rhythmical, as if Toby were jumping up and down.

"Hold there Burt. I know I'll find the damn thing in a minute. I thought it was on the pegboard here," Thompson said.

The squeak came faster until it was like a birdcall of sorts, a repetitious twisting of the metal spring against the wood frame of the old couch they had bought years ago at a house auction in Three Rivers, the town up in Michigan where Margaret's father grew up. Margaret had loved the couch at first sight and offered an unreasonable opening bid; when the bidding was in full swing, she refused to bow out and bought the couch for five hundred dollars. It had been worth about fifty, most said.

Burt glanced up once and pretended to examine the carpentry, holding his eyes on the greasy-looking slats.

"They no longer make floors with that method," he said. "It takes too much time and skill."

Clanking around in the bench drawer, Thompson didn't answer. He was beginning to wonder if the boy were jumping up and down on his feet, or his rear end. But his feet would hit a different spot each time on the davenport, missing the spring occasionally.

"Sure is nice outside," Burt said, his eyes to the window, shifting his big palms in his pockets.

Thompson slammed the drawer shut and felt the damp air of the basement tingle the sweat, a thin veneer, up and down the length of his spine. A breeze picked up outside and moved the rhubarb leaves.

The heavy smell of furnace oil left over from the winter mixed with the smell of laundry detergent, fabric softener, and lint.

"Jesus. I know where it is," Thompson said, picking at the back of his shirt. "It's in the damn toolbox in the garage."

Anxiously, Burt said, "I know where you keep it. I'll just grab it on the way back to my house."

"No. I'll go with you."

"No problem for me to just find it myself," he said.

"Sure, okay," he conceded. Margaret would be home any minute. She'd find the big man digging around in the garage.

He snapped the bench light out and the neon buzz was gone.

With a funny look on his face, as if he'd heard a great secret revealed, Burt went up the stairs first and left the house by the back door. In what Thompson thought was a gratuitous spectacle, he insisted on shaking hands goodbye. As he held his gray eyes on the minister's face, he said, in his hollow midwestern twang, "I thought you'd still be over to the church, but I'm glad to find you home Sundays for a change. Just my luck, really, because my points are off, and the old Chevy wears the worst for it."

"Thought I'd take a break today," Thompson said, moving away. Like an echo, the davenport squeak continued in his ear. "Sorry you missed Margaret."

"Shoot, I forgot the router bit. Forgot all about it. But I'll get it later. I'm not going to work down in the shop on a nice day like this, am I?"

"No," Thompson mumbled. "No. You're not."

In the sun parlor the boy was sitting silently, his legs dangling over the side of the davenport, the sun burnishing his blond hair, just as he had left him. He felt the tiny eyes follow him as he entered the room and sat down in the straightback chair.

"What were you doing up here?" he asked gently, changing tactics. He'd try the soft approach.

Toby did not move his eyes. Out the window, past the honeysuckle bush, Burt was in his own backyard, neck craned, looking up at the sky.

"Were you jumping up and down on the couch?"

Far back in the canal of his ear, against the drum, the sound of the spring still scratched and made his throat itch.

His back stuck to the cherry wood. Perhaps it was something new for the kid. Maybe he had just discovered it after all these years; all kids enjoyed the feel, like swinging on a swing or riding a bike or throwing a football in a long, perfect spiral.

Unflinching, his son continued to stare at him with his mouth open.

"Don't you have anything to say for yourself?" he said, wanting to shake the sound out of his head like water after a swim, to tilt over and pound the other side, or cram a swab in there to get at it. "That's all I'm asking you to do."

Gladys Jackson would wait for him until it became too late, and dangerous, near the end of her husband's afternoon shift at the factory.

When Toby moved his legs slightly, Thompson imagined he saw a small black stain on the inside of his thigh, but it was only a shadow of light from the window.

The words slipped gently from the boy's mouth. "I didn't think you'd be home this afternoon, Daddy." It was clear from the look on the boy's face, and the way he jerked his head away, that this was all he had to say on the matter.

"Well I'm here Toby," he said, backing away, moving past the chair and into the large double doorway where the sun, low enough now to have a reddish cast to it, the first early hints of twilight, burst directly into his eyes.

Something gave in the pit of his stomach. He felt un-qualified to talk with his son, as if he had lost his license to practice fatherhood.

In the living room all he could see was the shape of the boy against the light, a small dark movement of life.

The only place left for me, he thought, is back down in the basement with the sawdust of old projects, the ancient tools and the unaccusing wood. So he went through the kitchen and down the stairs, keeping the lights off, into the darkness. As before, the only light was from the low win-dow. Overhead he heard a soft padding sound as his son left the sun parlor and went upstairs to his room.

Thompson got up onto an old peach crate—one his fa-ther had used on the farm—for a direct view out of the win-dow. Brushing away cobwebs and small, tight bundles of spider eggs, he drew his eyes level with the grass in his yard. A few bugs flew in the white haze of twilight.

He felt the shame take root. Gladys's husband would be home from the plant. The day was ending. She'd mark this one against him. He'd owe her an explanation.

After a while Margaret came out of the garage. From his view he could see only her legs from the knees down. Strapped in her black high-heels, her ankles turned inward as if she were under a great weight. Her tan nylons sagged like an old neck. From the way she walked, he could tell she was carrying heavy bags of food from the store, one in each arm.

She'd take a turn talking to Toby. She wouldn't see what it might mean, that the boy might know something he shouldn't. And even if he had the truth, Thompson figured the child would hold it between his teeth, clutched there tight, like a forbidden object—that was something he'd count on.

Closer to the window he could make out the scuffs on the side of her shoes, the small point of the heel, a rubber pad on the tips, worn away at an angle. There was something important about what he was seeing, but he wasn't sure how. It was the angle and the place from which he was looking, he supposed. In the spring light, around the edges of the rhubarb leaves, draped in the sagging nylons, his wife's ankles were the most fragile things he had ever seen, ready to break, straining against the straps as she struggled to get through the screen door with both bags, under a heavy burden she carried without even knowing it.

Seed

I went home. I flew into the hot,
dried midwestern heart of summer.

My father stood by the airport gate with both hands dug
deep into his pockets, hunched over a bit, looking past me
over the hot tarmac where the plane waited, roasting in the
sun, to fly to some more productive part of the world. He
looked battered. The world was on his shoulders; you could
see that much; he was not strong, or proud, or really anything for that matter. He was just there, in a small town,
waiting for his son to return.

Clean and washed down, he smelled of soap and spice
cologne when we embraced, hard. He took me by the

shoulders and held me back and gave me a shake with both arms, as if testing my weight, to see if anything knocked about inside. Then he turned and walked us both across the small waiting room to the baggage area; all the while the heavy weight of his arm remained on my shoulder.

"Son," he said, looking at me and then turning back to watch for my bag.

"Dad," I returned, looking at his tan face. Skin sank down off his forehead and chin.

The luggage belt clanked so loud we didn't talk much. Dad didn't like to chat much about personal matters in public, anyway. So we stood silently waiting for my old army issue bag to push out from the metal flap door, a little piece of myself from New York arriving home.

It was his new car, an oversized Oldsmobile, white, with air conditioning and good stereo speakers in the back; it was so unlike him. Driving slowly, he took up the middle of the lane with the monstrous bulk.

Outside, through the heat, the town went past in silence. On the public golf course, dried to the color of burlap, where I ran my high school cross-country meets in the fall afternoons, a few diehards lugged their heavy bags through the heat. Past that, where a paper mill, brown and huge, had once stood, there was a low, gravelly patch of dust.

"Moved to Puerto Rico and cheap labor," my father explained. "Can you believe that? Puerto Rico. Making notebooks and typing paper down in that heat. The thought's enough to kill you."

The houses were obsessively neat and clean along the railway route that served the missing mill. Some had been upgraded and revamped enough so that even I noticed the difference, an additional wing tacked on, a new aluminum

shed in back. Each change I noticed added to my bewilder-
ment at how much I remembered. I knew each home in
some way. They were a part of me. And even the poorest
house in town was intact, still paintless, listing slightly to
one side, hoisted up with cinder blocks.

"Same family lives in that one," Dad explained, "that
lived there at least thirty years."

The only change was a satellite dish, strapped onto the
roof and held in place by long spiders of guy wires that
came down into the yard, a huge white shell opening to the
sky. Free television. A world of shows zoomed through
space to a small, hot town in Michigan. The free world for
the poor. Ears on roofs. I was home.

The last edge of sunlight sliced behind the garage and
low across the pebbled, dusty cement of the driveway. It
picked up each stone with light, raised a new texture to the
earth, turned the world above the ground hot white. Amid
the dried leaves and bush, our lawn was bright green under
a sprinkler. Green, glistening wet blades beneath a lazy curl
of water: our backyard, for the first time, flourished.

It was a small yard, rectangular in shape, about ten
yards wide and maybe twenty long, and it was bordered by
a white slat fence.

You could almost hear the chlorophyll throb, the cells
jangle under the falling water.

"Dad, the yard looks great," I said.

"Humm." He closed the car door and came out from
the oily smell of the garage and stood beside me quietly. He
didn't say a word about it, just stood and watched the
swoops of water.

Out back that evening, my father drank ice water from
his sweating glass while I nursed down a cold beer. We
were preparing to talk, to put words into the night air—no

easy task. The night music of crickets and small birds was on. Words were heavy. As if drinking a nice, dry martini, he brought the glass to his lips slowly and held it there for a moment, just letting the edge of water crest into his mouth.

A month ago he had called me and cried over the phone lines about the immense thirst he had for booze. His word: booze.

Now he talked in the night air. "Strange thing," he said.

"What's strange?"

"My dad could spot a minute hairline fracture on an X ray, his eyes were so sharp, even at the end, but he couldn't see enough to watch television or read the paper."

"He was a fine radiologist, Dad," I said.

"It's as if it kept him going like a small fire in his belly."

Grandfather had fought hard to keep his job at the hospital, right into senility. He paid his malpractice insurance until his death; listened to medical journals on tape; took yearly hunting trips to Canada with the Toledo Medical Association; even when he couldn't see enough to shoot a tree, he was hiding behind blinds and waiting for moose to wander by.

"He rode a horse to school," Dad said, and then he chuckled to himself.

The image of his father riding a horse pleased him.

"Old Blue."

Old Blue, the horse's name, seventy-five years later.

To make him linger, I thought, he would repeat that name for the rest of his life, a four-legged mantra. From my lips, the image would reach my child. It would outlast the evening air. It was a romantic thought, but it fit nicely into the clatter of insects and the lazy way my father sipped his ice water.

At the bottom of his glass were small white peas of ice.

He tipped it back, tapped the bottom of the glass with one finger and let them slide into his mouth.

"I have to rake the mulch down near the roots in the front yard," he said. "If you don't rake fresh-mown mulch into the roots it only serves to block out the sun rays from the blades."

"I haven't seen the front yard, yet," I answered.

"It needs some nitrates for the roots, to last the winter."

"I could use some nitrates," I said. The laugh didn't come. It wasn't a matter for joking, I sensed. Sternly, he looked across the yard into the dark bushes.

For many reasons it didn't seem strange that he was talking about things like nitrates, that they would block out the sun. But if there had been enough light in the backyard that night—just a purple twilight haze of light—I might have seen the despair in his eyes.

Later, we left for our walk down the back alley and circled behind the houses and garages to the front of the block. Lumbering along, he swung his legs forward in an old man's walk, I thought, until I noticed that I too stepped forward in the same way and took up the sidewalk with the swing of my legs.

We passed familiar homes, varied architecture, colonials crammed against bungalows and Victorians.

"She needed a rest from me," he had told me a week before my visit, through the clarity of optical phone fibers. I could almost feel his lips brushing my ear.

Now I wanted explanations the way the state needed rain. In the Midwest, motivation comes from standing back from something, from moving far away from it. Out East, we would push head on into the problem, face it with a barrage of confrontations, with the logical, scientific methods of psychotherapy, or some such concoction. My father just let my mother go, and my mother gladly left. She shoved away from him as if in a boat, pushing hard so the hull would not slam against the dock.

When we got back to the house my father went to bed, and I sat outside and let the questions move through me. For some reason the crickets became silent. I imagined I could hear the grass calling for water, the dry crops hoping for rain, the sprinkler out front answering with a hiss. In the eaves of the house next door there was the soft purring of some sleeping bird, a sound that seemed so pure it gave any meaning the mind wanted for it, and none.

The Olds stank inside of new vinyl, Dad's Spice, and my own weary morning breath. He moved the steering wheel a lot to keep the big car on course. I was blurry-eyed from my lack of sleep.

He was telling me an old story about our neighbor, Frank, who went on his annual corporate fly fishing trip to Canada with the usual batch of television network executives from New York, and the local affiliate men from various small towns. The idea behind the trip was to get up into the backcountry and mingle together, drinking beer, fishing, making deals, gaining a better sense of togetherness. But it didn't always work. A clash of one kind or another happened every year and Frank relished, each in a new way, these confrontations of culture and class.

"So that big-wig anchorman, you know the one does the nightly news. He arrives late all decked out in a clean white shirt still creased from the dry cleaners, chinos, a brand spankin' new Orvis fishing vest that had never seen the light of day."

Dad was excited because this story solidified his feelings about fancy East Coast types.

"And to top it off he's got himself a very expensive pair

of hip waders. Imported from France or something, if there is such a thing."

I could guess the punch line, but I let him go on anyway.

"Finally, he had this very expensive graphite rod that must've cost him an arm and leg and it's nice stuff. But it's a damn spincasting rod. And when he's up there, far up, in the damn canoe, he gets the thing out of the case and the other guys just sit there and stare, plug-eyed at him. Not a single fly on him. Only this big, ugly, classless spincasting rod."

That was the end of story. Smiling, he drove on.

"Isn't that something? The man thought he could buy himself into an outdoorsman. My father would have had something to say about that one, wouldn't he."

A wide span of hot asphalt bibbed the True Value Hardware Center, space enough for a few hundred cars. Next to it, a supermarket sprawled, hammered flat by the sky.

Dad selected a spot near the door and guided the monster deftly between the yellow lines.

"She runs smooth, doesn't she?" he said as the engine clicked, sputtered, then died out.

I could feel the heat outside working into the car, the sun beginning to bake the smooth seats like a Teflon pan.

He walked surefooted down the long aisle, past rakes hanging in rows from brackets, displays of artificial brick surfacing, life-size cutouts of women with toothy smiles holding cans of paint into the air.

At the end of the aisle, he turned right and walked past a whole room of hanging lamps, chandeliers, and fake Tiffany. Beyond this, in the very back, the store opened up into a warehouse. Natural light came down from skylights.

Hewn beams gave it a barnlike feel. Bulging stacks of mulch and humus, seed and fertilizer steamed in a dank room.

Dad took a deep breath. There was the potential for life in the air. He began to study the bags carefully. He lifted some from the piles to read the fine print. Some were just plain brown bags. Others had bright green grass photographed on the paper wrapping.

The stench of processed manure was starting to make me sick, but after a while he made his selection—a plain brown, enough seed for a football field.

"Seed on well-raked soil," he read in a deep, sermonizing voice. "Early morning hours are preferable."

The bag flopped down. "That's the seed I need. Always take the second one down because it will be dryer than the one on top or the ones near the bottom." This was his philosophy. He took the second one down everywhere: ice cream cartons, the paper at the newsstand, a box of cereal, a new car.

With the bag hugged to his chest he hobbled out of the room.

The cashier smiled at him in a knowing way.

"Another bag of seed," she said, tapping the keys with her fingernails. "You must be planting a lot."

"You remember?" my father said.

"Oh, sure. A sack of Lawn Guard fertilizer and a fifty-pound sack of seed, and a red spreader. Lug nuts, screws, wallpaper—I remember it all. Have to in this line of business."

"Kentucky bluegrass is good stuff," he said over the mull of the engine. "It's tough and it grows nice and smooth." On a sheet of velvet, a layer of raw air, we were moving down the street. Air conditioning roared from the vents.

"Dad, you never cared much about the lawn before."
"Well, I do now."
"I noticed that, Dad."
"You did, did you? That's good."

"Slide over," he ordered when he got out of the car and stood in the heat. "Pop the trunk." Already his face was sweaty. His jowls jiggled beneath his mouth and his face seemed pulled down by the heavy gravity of this earth: He was old, tired looking, and his eyes looked over the roof of the car, at the lawn.

Then he went around behind the car and opened the trunk. After some thudding about, as if wrestling with a body back there, he came back around to the window with the seed bag draped over his shoulder in a fireman's carry, breathing hard, his eyes firm, dark black, resolute. Although he looked old, he also looked ruddy and brown-skinned, cowboyish, with determined wrinkles over his brows and his slicked-down hair.

"Run on to the store and grab some lunch, maybe something for dinner too. I'm anxious to get on with this seeding."

I drove around for a while, taking streets at random, moving through the dried-out air. There was time to kill, time to move through, to take back and reclaim.

There were lakes that I didn't remember, each low in water, rimmed with dried mud. There were more homes, more split-levels built into hillsides, and more condos where fields once stood; a whole field riddled with roads that spread out like the veins in a leaf, all ending in cul-de-sacs.

People wanted an end to things, a dead end, an end of the line, I thought. They needed a place to turn around from, to return back into the world. The answer to that need is the cul-de-sac.

Two years away and the trees seemed torn away. Further out of town, where the blueberry crops grew and there were rows of corn, usually, the land was obviously dying from the lack of rain. Great clouds of dust were blown across the road. There were long pipe sprinklers left out across the fields, shaped like a long sawhorse—useless. A tractor drew some implement across the land, stirring more dust. When I got fifteen miles worth of these things, I made a U-turn (kicking still more dust) and headed back.

From New York I had called my mother and told her that I was on my way out to visit. She didn't say much, just that he needed to see me, and that she would not be around anymore. Spend some quality time with your father, she suggested. Maybe you can work some sense into the man if you try hard enough.

Quality time: a funny way to put it. To work sense into someone made me think of kneading bread.

Where will you be, exactly? I pried.

She was going north for a while with Aunt Dorris, probably for the rest of the summer if not longer, depending for the most part on Dorris's plans.

In Petoskey, a town way up near the tip of the state, she would play endless games of pinochle on the veranda of the inn, a holdover from the big days of northern Michigan when the rich from Chicago steamered up Lake Michigan for the summer. They would mark score with stubby little pencils, adding things up, pretending to be competitive about their luck. But it would remain just luck, and they'd get tired of it the way Mom got tired of Dad.

At all costs they wouldn't mention his name, or his drinking, or the way he broke five ribs when he tumbled down the stairs, drunk, so full of the stuff that he didn't feel a single bone crack.

And at night up there the air would get cold enough for frost, from Canada, but she would sleep under a mound of Hudson Bay blankets and feel the immense security of her own body heat, the reassuring furnace of heart and skin that reminds you of your own life, of the womb, of every single deep, cold winter night you ever lived through as a child and alone as an adult.

"I left him because I didn't know what else to do," she told me, near the end of the conversation. "At times the only way to get out is to get out."

Was this wisdom running deep tendrils into the mid-western sod? Were these thoughts born out of log cabins and famine, waxed paper windows and the oily sooty light of a whale oil lamp? "The only way to get out is to get out." You pick up the family and move West because, well, sometimes you just have to do what you have to do. Sitting in New York that night, I thought about the way this country was founded on such convoluted, in-turning, snake-eating-its-tale phrases. No guts, glory, pride, oppression, stagecoach dreaming drive: just routine, run-of-the-mill phrase turning.

Half our backyard was gone. That much I could see from the driveway. When I got out of the car and went to the fence, I saw Dad holding on to a Rototiller machine, cutting up the sod, pulling it up in big hunks and then pushing it under again. Gas fumes yellowed the air. Pulled along as if by a dog, he held on. The engine gave a moan when it grabbed onto fresh grass, the growl from the back of a dog's throat. Where the grass had been there was a raw, open swath of black dirt that sucked up the sunlight and color.

I ran behind him. Through his shirt I could see the flesh of his back jiggling and bouncing with the machine.

"Jesus Christ," I yelled, putting one hand on his shoulder. He pulled a lever and silence crumpled down on us like a loose stage curtain that smelled of lawn and gas and the burning earth. Birds were clicking in the trees, and wrenches clanged on the cement floor in our neighbor's garage, and, several houses down, the drone of a lawn-mower as it neatened a yard.

He stood like a dirty field hand with his machine and mumbled "Son" in a low voice.

I was looking at his footprints waffled on the humus, perfect, like Neil Armstrong's prints on the moon, left behind from some other age and time. They'd stay there forever, I thought, if I let them.

"What am I going to do?" he said. A light choke and he began to cry to himself. The tears began to emerge slowly.

I took hold of his elbow and then cradled him completely in my arms. He drew himself up into his sobs, folded over in my arms.

For a minute I let him go on like this. Then, as if guiding a blind man, I grabbed the back of his elbow, stood slightly behind him, and helped him over to the patio.

He settled in the chair. Our eyes met. I sat down too.

"How am I going to make it?" he said.

"I'm not sure."

"This place."

"Yeah." I understood. I left "this place." "This place" hurt before I understood why. Now I know why.

"Frank took me flying last week, along the river to Lake Michigan and then down a ways towards Chicago. Even the Sleeping Bear dunes looked dead from way up. The razor grass is brown, gone."

"Move to New York, Dad. You can live with me until you find a place, a new job. Begin again."

His smile said yes and it said no. Without turning away or speaking, he let me know that too much told him we could not and should not live together. The tight bonds, the two magnets that pole to pole repel until they flip around and attract like the migration patterns of trout and birds and whales.

It was late evening, Saturday night. Cars drag raced two blocks away. We could hear them at the red light as they roared engines and prepared to go.

"I had an offer to teach at Cornell," he was explaining to me. I could just see his mouth move in the darkness. "And we decided against it for many reasons. Believe it or not, we were in love with this place. It was perfect. Nights like these we would come up here just to take walks under these trees."

We had steaks on the grill. They popped and sizzled and sent flames up into Dad's clean, white oxford shirt.

"We stayed," he concluded.

Earlier, we had returned the tiller to the rental place; tied it down into the trunk and drove there slowly. I took the machine in while he waited outside in the car, on the passenger side, hidden in the glare of the windshield. Behind the counter the clerk eyed me in a suspicious manner while I explained to him that my father was sick and I wanted to bring it back a week early. He refused. I didn't fight. I paid the week's rent, took the receipt and went back to the car.

The evening drugged us, the rhythmic click of the earth going into low gear, changing course. A darkness you could depend on cradled us and drew her fingers up beneath the eyes and the mind.

"Thanks for helping me reseed that mess," he said.

"I hope it comes back nicely.'

"Know why I think I did that?" he said, approaching each word with hesitation.

"No, why Dad?"

"Because the perfect stuff sometimes has to be uprooted

and changed; no matter how good it is, it grows even better the second time around."

"But, Dad, you were heading into a third time, a third uprooting and a third change. And all that takes energy and time."

"I have plenty of both," he said, tipping back the bottle of nonalcoholic beer, popping it from his lips with the sound of sucking air.

"I guess you do."

"Time to kill," he sighed.

Back in New York I had a dream. Mom was in the backyard speaking to Dad. Her hair was purple, a great mane down to her knees, as dark as the soil Dad was planting. She was begging him for something, but he wasn't listening. His eyes were down on the lawn, on his foot kicking the clods of dirt. She moved close, face to face, and began moving her mouth over words until he looked up at her and smiled. His face was new. His jowls were gone. The tears dripped down to the soil. One seed of grass miraculously split open and entered the world a full-grown blade of Kentucky blue a half inch tall. Together they sat in the dirt and watched. The midwestern sky was a loose tarpaulin of haze. They lay down under it and watched night come. It came with answers, many of them, and with the full throat of sounds. When it was almost dark, they stood up and held hands. There were many crickets and birds all singing together, a chorus of dead wings rubbing. There were plenty of stars through the haze. At least for a moment, the place was perfect again.

A Quick
Kiss
of
Redemption

When I was stuck in my room to think about it, all I could muster at first was the dry smell of limestone, organ dust, and the raw bitter taste of God in our mouths. Sure enough, we were up as high as we could get with the big man himself, or at least that's how I construed it. Long before I was sent to my room, I was fed a lot of lines regarding the subject of God, "correct behavior," being a good boy. The whole thing triggered an outbreak of head shaking around me. All those heads shaking as if I were some sad, sad case, the kind of guy God just forgot about—a mad, twisting, wild-horse-of-a-guy in need of whipping and corralling and breaking in. Truth is, in the rebellion department I hardly fit the bill: In fact I was just a beginner. Lying on my bed, feeling the damp fall air slink under the windowsill, I began to wonder if God might indeed be shaking his big, fat head at me—shaking, shaking away as if the words were stuck in his mouth and he had, finally, after making the whole universe and doling out judgments through two world wars, finally met his match in me, Rudy Stanwick.

Basically, the whole thing began when Max Gilheart discovered the stairway up to the top of the sanctuary during our Sunday morning confirmation class. Max was a diabolical guy, always pulling somebody into trouble and then wresting himself out of it—a moral Houdini. He gained his confidence from his two older brothers, who outperformed him by a mile. But he was the only guy in the class of five, so I made do with him. I found out later that Max's brother, Rob, who had been through the two-year program already, had discovered the stairway a long time ago and passed the information on to his brother. Max was careful to make it look like his exclusive find. Max wore his clip-on bow tie and a shiny polyester suit. With his usual, angelic, chubby-cheek face, he was fooling around as he led me out into the hall.

During the breaks, our teacher, Mr. Lewis, tended to spend an inordinate amount of time with the girls; usually, recently, answering profound questions about the book of Job. You know: Why did Job suffer so damn much—stuff like that. So Max and I hung out, guzzled apple cider, and discussed our cars, dates, football, whatever mindless subject came to mind.

"This is serious shit, man," he said once his upper lip was clean. "I mean I've been meaning to show you this."

There were two doors in the hall. One went into a

janitorial storage closet that held the chlorine smell of cleansing powder along with the moldy algae tang of half-dry mop heads. Once, Max and I hid in the closet and listened to the top-forty countdown on an old, paint-splattered G.E. transistor radio—the hits from coast to coast, every damn one of them. That door held no surprises. The other door—I tested it once before, sliding my palm casually across the knob during a break—was, as far as anyone knew, locked tight.

But Max began to work the knob, jiggling it like mad as he pulled back on the door.

A nice tight click of tumblers falling, and he got the door open.

"Holy," he said as we let our eyes adjust. The tiny room was weakly illuminated by gray, wet light coming through a frosted window. Bracketed against the wall was a black iron ladder that ascended up into a square hole in the ceiling; beyond that hole was a black void, black on top of black.

Temptation comes in strange forms; and maybe nothing is truly more appealing to the human heart than a ladder leading up into a black void—I don't know. What I do know is that Max and I were breathing hard while Mr. Lewis's voice mulled and pondered outside the door, calling for us.

"We'd better go back," Max said.

"Why?"

"Because I don't want to go up there now. If we stay here any longer, we'll be stuck out here through the rest of class. If Mr. Lewis sees us coming out he'll have the lock on this thing fixed and we'll never be able to . . ." Max's voice faded.

About as long as we could, we stood pondering the implications of the ladder, testing our hearts against the ripe darkness to which it led. A good ladder says climb me. But Max began to fidget. He gave off a bitter nervous odor that mixed with his antiperspirant. His plastic heels kept clicking against the tile floor. Soon, he opened the door and slipped out into the hall and I followed behind, unwilling to face temptation alone.

Back in class I thought about a lot of things as Lewis explained how God decided to test Job's faith. Mr. Lewis ran a chain of pharmacy stores around town and never failed to connect his lessons with his profession. This time he was going on about the FDA and God; how in his own field of work he was held accountable to the FDA for everything he did, just like we are held accountable to God.

I looked over at Max and he was casting Sally Hoops a long, blatant stare. Sally looked right back and in return, gestured obscenely with her finger.

Because she had pierced ears and hung out with a boy whose nickname was Oily, Sally was imbued with a notorious aura—she dared you to try something; and you knew she had tried it all. Yet there she was, butt planted firmly on her folding chair, face cast up at Lewis with a kind of rough, pious concern.

Droning on, Mr. Lewis was hitting full stride. But who was listening?

"Excuse me sir," I suddenly said.

Balding Lewis slapped his knees and moved forward. "Yes?"

"Why was God always testing, messing with people's minds and stuff? I mean he was always taking things away and then returning them. By today's standards that's kind of nasty, you know. I mean it stinks, really."

Big sigh. Lots of self-control.

"Rudy, I'm not even going to answer that, son. Why?

you might ask. Well, I'll tell you. Rudy, you've been in this class for over a year now, readying yourself for membership in this church. In all that time, you have had plenty of opportunities to ask a question. Now, at last, after all that time, you come out with this—this inappropriate tone.''

Then he asked me to step out of the classroom and think about what I had said. So I went back out to the hallway, looked out the window for a while at the wild, wet fall weather, and then went down the stairs to the main foyer where people were coming in to church.

Lots of big, fat Buicks were swinging up to the door, expelling loads of infirm old ladies. I liked these old ladies. For one thing, they were hopeful the way they struggled into the building with their chrome walkers, canes, and such, battling the swinging doors and the slope of the sidewalk; all of them with their big, puffy dresses and hair nets; and they smiled in the crinkled, tight way of survivors, of war-weary soldiers joyously coming home.

Most impressive to me was the fact that all their husbands and lovers were dead. All the men were gone. Yet they got up, made breakfast dutifully, puffed powder on their faces, popped their teeth in, and, against the great arthritic anguish traveled to church—as if men were just a stage in their life to live through. I thought about those men, about all the six-packs they had at one time downed during *Monday Night Football;* about their cussing and anger; about the way they screwed around with other women. I thought about the way they probably died off: Some saw their livers go. Others drove too fast. Even more were consumed by their own anger or remorse.

I think these ladies knew I loved them. Up they came to squeeze my cheeks and talk, even though I was half hidden back near the coat closet.

"Your sister, sweet," Edith Larson, an old family friend

asked, "is she still in the hospital?" It wasn't a question I wanted to hear, but I was glad she asked. Nobody else did.

"Umm humm," I said.

Brittle fingers around my arm. She leaned against me. Inside her wrinkled, twisted face, her eyes were all watery and young.

"They'll take good care of her up there," she whispered, knowingly, coming close. And I believed she did know.

"Don't fret," she whispered and was gone, tottering into the sanctuary, leaning against the metal of her walker.

Max came up.

"Hey, dude, nice going," he said, holding out his palm for the slap I refused to give him.

"I couldn't handle it," I said.

"Yeah, man, I know exactly where you're coming from. I mean I didn't think too much about it, but, what the hell." Max's clip-on bow tie hung down from one metal clasp. I let it hang.

Sally walked by just then. When she got past me, she cocked her head a little and made a nice smile. Her fresh lipstick terrible in the light. Her hair swung just right. Oily or not, I was starting to like her; or maybe she was starting to like me.

"Sally," I said.

"Yeah." She turned and came up to me. Max took a step back, fading.

"How're you doing?"

"Fine," she sang, the word hanging out there to dry.

Closer, I saw a few pimples up above her eyebrows, covered over by masking cream. I liked that. Her lips went slightly apart as she mulled a piece of gum slowly, exposing sharp white teeth against bright pink gums.

"Lewis sure was P.O.'d at you," she said. "You left and

he couldn't hardly talk. Not that I was listening to him, you know."

She swung when she talked, her body brushed against the fabric of her skirt. I could almost hear it. She did a complete turn, casting a glance at the door for her mother who would be arriving. My brain slowed her motion down and got a good look at her backside, her butt. Again, there was the imagined sound of flesh against fabric, the static of her panties catching the back of her skirt as it flowed over it.

She said, "You know, it was really cool what you said. I mean, I wanted to say the same thing."

"Well, if you liked it that much, I'll do it again sometime," I said.

Just a fraction of an inch closer, she moved. From beneath her blouse came a flowery smell.

"It's such a fucking crime," she said. "I mean I don't believe all this junk, but I sit through it anyway. I mean, you know."

She did another turn. I did know.

Max was across the room with a frightened look on his face. I knew what he was thinking. Sally displayed herself around school in skintight jeans and shirts tied up so her belly button showed. Oily was her main boyfriend, but sometimes you'd see her giving some other guy a sloppy wet kiss in the hallway. And everyone knew what a horrible mess of a family she had. Her old man went on and off the payroll at Checker Cab Company, depending on his drinking and the union; her older sister had been messed up in a car accident. On top of all that, her mother pressed charges against her father for molesting her younger sister. After that, her folks split up. Now her mom worked the checkout at 7-Eleven, where everyone could see her.

"Well, see ya," she said, spinning away, casting one little forlorn smile over her shoulder.

Timid Max came back over on tiptoes. "Hey, hey, hey," he said. "You'd better watch yourself."

"You'd better watch this," I said, lifting a fist to his nose.

"No problem," he said, wary, his clip-on tie hanging from a silver clasp.

A pretty dull week came between that Sunday and the next. Things did happen, but nothing too interesting in the scheme of things. God, or whatever, pelted the state with cold rain through Wednesday. When it stopped Thursday morning all the trees were cold and naked and the leaves plastered over everything. Because Dr. Lewis called my old man about my "worrisome" behavior, Dad, who felt the need to hand out some kind of punishment—although he smiled when he did it—said there was a rake with my name on it in the garage.

Sentenced to a Saturday of hard labor, I raked with joy. The air was cool, the leaves were heavy. I put the game on the radio. Blisters appeared on each of my fingers.

Together we stood in the half-darkness looking at that ladder.

"Wow," she said the way I hoped she would.

Outside, donut break was in full swing.

With her, the room became smaller, closer, darker. In the dim light, her hair was as fine as cobwebs. I caught a whiff of it when she was close enough—strawberry, ripe, sweet, like bubble gum.

With a nonchalant ease she had slipped right into my plan. From a big tube that said Bonne Bell, she put lip gloss on, pursed them. They shined like mirrors. "Let's go," she said simply.

At first in the closet it was too dark to see her mouth. A loose skirt swayed over her hips, this one darker and tweedy and stuck closed with a big brass safety pin. Beneath her white blouse, flowers bloomed as far as my nose was concerned.

"Let's go up," I said.

"Where does it go?"

"Above the sanctuary, I think."

"Okay." She sighed and raised both arms up.

I braced my feet on the bottom rung, grabbed one above me, and yanked back to test my weight. I began the climb up into the darkness.

As I followed the ladder up through the heart of the pipe organ I could taste the old dust moving about me. Sally's soft breath rose and fell beneath my feet.

I should have known. With the taste of desire and excitement in my mouth and the way light slid down the big copper pipes like water—good, natural light—there were dangerous forces working in me.

When I broke open into the pure light of the sanctuary it was onto a small ledge over the organ, above the choir boxes and pulpit and all of that stuff, way up, in the curved arches of the ceiling, almost at the pinnacle of the stained glass windows.

Sally emerged from the darkness showing a good long stretch of her legs. There wasn't much space to move around in, about two yards until a small curled lip of stone came up into a wall. But we had room to stretch out in, and we did.

Below us a church service was shaping up. Sally took a peek over the edge.

"What'dy see?"

"Just McCutchy setting things up," she whispered, her face rainbowed as hell in the colored lights from a stained glass window, one I'd always wanted to see up close. In it two carpenters were working a long saw, tearing into a big log or something, backs heaving into it. Up close, details were all choppy and you could see how broken up it all was in a deceptive sort of way; but you could still make out the straining muscles of their backs which were a different color brown, more of a tannish brown.

"Oh Rudy, you're right," Sally said after I told her what they were doing.

"This beats listening to old Lewis, doesn't it?" I said.

"God, it's great up here."

"Not quite heaven, but almost."

She rolled on her back and looked up at the ceiling. Glossy blond and fanned out, her hair begged to be stroked. A few wandering strands itched my cheek.

Max was probably right, I thought. Sally was nothing but real, honest-to-God trouble. Facts were facts. Oily—after all—did have a tattoo on his arm of a devil face, and under it the words "eat shit and die." But any fears I had of Oily were blown away by a big puffing sound, a click of wooden stops, and a wheezing, pumping as the organ began to ready itself.

"Oh boy," I said. "They're gonna play the FDA theme song for Lewis."

Loud enough to shake our ribs, a little ditty began at a couple of hundred decibels.

She turned against me, moved close, and parted her hair like a couple of curtains and presented her face to me. Up close, her eyes were painfully blue, as sharp as broken bottles. Her lips were abused, crinkled and cracked. Slightly apart, I could see her nicotined teeth. Above the plucked ridge of her brow, the pimple from last week was gone, but the skin was scarred in many places with tiny pocks.

Through the organ prelude we shoved our lips together, kissing recklessly. The taste of her mouth was bubble gum and stale smoke.

The music stopped and the air was filled with the din of human movement. A microphone popped on—static, up close, near our heads. A good solid tap tested the buzzing amplifiers. Pews were filling below—families all happy, joyous, ready to serve God. Robed processors were collecting in the back, readying for the march. Sally's mother probably sat, alone, waiting to sing.

We both felt so lonely and helpless amid the cold implication of that sacred space, the cool arch of the limestone ceiling. That's why we went at it so heavy; her lips working hard against mine, our teeth clicking like marbles.

The opening hymn came and went. Shuffling feet echoed like a broom sweeping. By that time, Sally's hand was wedged down the back of my underwear, just resting on the ridge of my rear end. One of her hip bones was hard against me.

The Lord's Prayer was recited.

Then a pause, a quick organ introduction, and McCutchy began his sermon, a great booming voice that seemed meaningless and fuzzy.

Something made her stop kissing me, prop her head on her palm, and undo, with one hand, the first two buttons of her blouse.

"Umm humm," she said, smiling.

Then one more button until the lace cup of her bra lay exposed in the clear air.

I lost my mind. I reached up to touch. There was the music of the organ again kicking out "Onward Christian Soldiers," with the choir taking the first stanza and then the whole sloppy place kicking in. As the music ended I was still just moving into that strange, soft territory of flesh. At that moment all the bells of sin roared loud in my ears, I swear that is true; each one of my fingers carried the guilt of the others as they moved under that flap of cotton.

Perhaps it was the guilt that made her laugh, or just the tickle of my fingers, or the shock of my own passion. Or maybe the sudden end of the song just lifted up a vial of sound and left us out there alone in the silence.

Sally's peal of giggles probably sounded for an instant like angelic spirits haunting the upper vault of the church.

A sort of mild response came from below—breezy whispers in the congregation.

I tried to cover her mouth. Giggles turned into a wild snorting of hot air behind my fingers.

A sort of dull chill ran through me. I began to think about the sadness in Sally's face, the scars she had; I began to think about all the old ladies who had struggled and the way pain came through their sagging skin, their fragile bones; I began to think of all of the times I had felt laughter at my back and turned only to find smug hidden smiles; I began to think of the way Oily carved his initials into each one of his knuckles and the things he would eventually do to Sally: and the guys who were willing to beat me to a pulp because I just happened to exist the way I did. It made me happy that all of those judgmental sinners below could relish the joy I felt, join me in a good laugh. For all I cared at that instant they could take the collection plate and pass it up to me coinless, dusty, full of hate. And so I let loose a big laugh. One single "h—a—a" that bounced "h—a—a" from one wall "h—a—a" to the back "h—a—a" into the microphone and back "a—a—a."

As if in response, the organ kicked in again, a little trill at the top of the scale and then one low blast that shook our bones and made us collect ourselves into one last, long kiss—the absolute last one, her hand up at the nape of my neck, mine down in the strong arch of her spine.

The ladder took us down into the loud roaring pipes of the organ.

"Wow," Sally said at the bottom, her voice squeaky, different, putting fingers in her ear and shaking her hair around. "What a head trip."

That was all it came down to—a head trip in a Brooks Brothers blazer and argyle socks. To her I was just another one of the multitudinous heady experiences that made up her life, a ride over a different roller coaster, yet another guy.

"That was nice," she said to me before she went down the stairs. I wanted to read her eyes. I wanted something to last. I wanted to be lonely and angry with her.

She went down first, alone, to avoid suspicion. As she swayed down the stairs, I felt an urge to shout some brilliant, significant thing to her; but I didn't; the words were gone that once explained what we did or what made us do it.

I mixed into the after-church mingling. All around the head shaking was beginning. Everyone was doing it. Nodding and shaking, working sin around in their mouths like a bad taste. Only Max stayed away from me, shielded between his mother and father like a little prince in his suede Hush Puppies, holding his mother's hand. His wry grin had me pegged. It should've told me everything.

I walked up to him anyway.

"Max, how're you doing?"

"Fine, Rud. You missed a great second half of class." He winked.

"I'll bet."

"We solved all the world's problems and added a few."

"Right."

"Oh, Dad, I'll be right there. Hey, Rudy, stay out of trouble, will you?" He cast me that smile again.

"Sure dirt breath," I said after him. He left the stench of old roll-on and the straw smell of singed polyester. That was it for Max; he was history to me, gone, not worth the trouble.